THE MEDWAY YEARS

PROLOGUE — "The River"

Before the years carried them in different directions—before the heartbreaks, the fights, the weddings, the mistakes, the letters that crossed oceans— they were simply kids on the banks of the River Medway.

They didn't think of themselves as lucky or doomed or destined   for   anything. They were just boys and girls in hand-me-down coats, pockets full of hopes too big for their streets, eyes bright with the certainty that the world was waiting for them.

On warm evenings, they'd gather by the river, skipping stones, sharing secrets, planning futures they could barely imagine. The tide moved slowly then, gentle, sure, as if promising them time. Time to grow, time to choose, time to become whoever they believed they might be.

None of them knew how quickly that time would pass.

The river outlasted all of it— the music from Riverview Hall that drifted across the water, the laughter that echoed down the lanes, the friendships that tightened and frayed, the loves that sparked, faded, or were carried too far away.

THE MEDWAY YEARS

Years later, when they looked back, they would say it began there— in the shadow of the dockyard cranes, in the glow of streetlamps turning the water gold, in the simple belief that growing up would be easy.

But the river always knew better.

It watched them step into their lives— together, then apart— and waited quietly to see who would find their way home again.

THE MEDWAY YEARS

CHAPTER ONE – MEDWAY, EARLY 1960s

The Medway towns of 1961 sat in that quiet space between the old world and the new. The war had ended more than fifteen years earlier, yet you could still feel its aftershocks in the cracked brickwork, the patched-up roofs, and the way older folks still measured life in "before the war" and "after." But for the young—kids who had grown up knowing only peace—there was a restless sense that something bigger was coming.

The **dockyards** were the heart of the place, thumping with the clang of metal on metal, the hiss of steam, and the calls of men who'd been working there since before anyone in the group was born. Ships rose like giants above the rooftops, their grey hulls catching the weak Kentish sunlight. For the boys who wanted a trade, the dockyard was the obvious path; for those who didn't, its looming presence was a reminder of what they might end up doing if they didn't find something better.

The **streets were tight terraces**, narrow front gardens filled with washing lines, bicycles, and kids' chalk drawings. Everyone knew everyone else. If you sneaked home late, your mum knew before you walked through the door. If a couple argued, the neighbours heard it through the thin walls. And in summer, when the windows were pushed open and the scent of cut grass mixed with cigarette smoke from the corner pub, the whole neighbourhood felt like one long, shared conversation.

THE MEDWAY YEARS

Saturday nights belonged to the **dance halls**—glorious, sweaty places where the lights were low, the music loud, and the world felt full of possibility. Vinyl spun on crackling record players, American rock 'n' roll cutting through the air, and the floorboards vibrated under the weight of kids who'd worked all week and needed somewhere to feel alive. Here, romances sparked, fizzled, or flared into drama; here, glances meant something; here, the Medway youth could become the people they imagined themselves to be.

Work was changing too. The older generation prized **apprenticeships**—solid, respectable trades in carpentry, bricklaying, electrical work, engineering. But the new world was creeping in, offices, telephones, motorcars, the first whispers of a different kind of future. Some boys grabbed at these changes with both hands. Others drifted, uncertain, drifting from job to job, hoping something would "turn up."

The girls were no different. Some were keen to settle, dreaming of their own small houses and tidy lives. Others yearned for something wider than the Medway streets, something beyond the dockyard gates and the predictable routines of their parents.

Underneath it all lay a subtle but undeniable optimism. The older generation still pinched pennies, still saved string and reused jars, and told stories of rationing. But the young? They were hungry for laughter, for music, for late buses home from dances. The world was shifting—slowly, quietly—and they could feel it in their bones.

This was the Medway of their youth: **half old, half new, familiar yet full of promise**. A place where friendships were

THE MEDWAY YEARS

forged on street corners, where romances rose and fell like the tide, and where the future was a path no one had yet walked.

Saturday Night at The Riverview

The **Riverview Dance Hall** always came alive before the sun had even finished setting. Its windows glowed with warm yellow light, spilling onto the pavement like a promise. Music thrummed against the glass—Elvis tonight, by the sound of it—and every few minutes the doors opened to release a burst of laughter, cigarette smoke, and excitement into the cooling air.

Dougie Barnes stood near the entrance, hands in his jacket pockets, watching the trickle of people arriving. The river behind the hall was quiet, a slow-moving ribbon catching the last of the day's light, but inside the place was buzzing with life. Brenda slipped her arm through his.

"You're not thinking of going home early, are you?" she teased.

"Me?" Dougie said. "Not a chance."

He smiled, though truthfully he wasn't sure what kind of night he was in for. The group hadn't been together like this in a while, and whenever that happened, the energy always felt unpredictable—like weather that could turn at any moment.

A shout cut through the music spilling from the hall. "Dougie, you miserable sod! You're early!"

THE MEDWAY YEARS

Barry Medhurst strode up the pavement with Jackie Pellet clinging happily to his arm. Barry looked like he could lift the dance hall on his shoulders if he had to; Jackie bounced beside him like she had springs in her shoes.

"Early?" Dougie said. "You lot are late."

"We're stylishly timed," Jackie said, grinning as she flicked a curl from her eyes. "There's a difference."

Before Dougie could reply, Tony Marks and Maggie Heston appeared, walking in as if the world were a spotlight.

Tony, tall and sharp, caught sight of them and raised a hand. Maggie—pretty as a picture in her powder-blue dress—leaned into him with an easy familiarity that made Brenda glance away, as if intruding on something private.

"All right, lads?" Tony called.

"Evening," Maggie added with a warm smile.

They gathered in a loose circle, the usual greetings overlapping nods, jokes, compliments about dresses or jackets. The kind of small talk that always came before the real energy of the night. Then Martin Prentice arrived.

"Ladies and gentlemen!" he announced grandly, stepping onto the pavement like an actor taking the stage. "Fear not. The entertainment has *finally* arrived."

"About time," Barry said. "We were running out of people to laugh at."

"Oh, Barry," Martin replied with a dramatic sigh, "there's always *you*."

THE MEDWAY YEARS

Laughter rippled through the group. Even Brenda cracked a smile.

Two more figures approached from across the road—Brian Batchelor with his easy swagger, and Maureen West close behind, her expression somewhere between fondness and caution.

Brian slapped Kevin Powers on the back as the football-mad lad jogged to catch up with June Pearton, who followed a pace behind, smoothing her skirt as if she were already bracing for whatever madness Kevin might get up to.

"All here then?" Kevin asked, a little breathless.

"Looks like it," Tony said. "Good turnout."

A moment settled over them, one of those small, quiet spaces between laughter and movement. The lot of them stood there, framed by the glow of the dance hall behind and the drifting river light ahead—young, hopeful, a little uncertain, but bound together by years of shared streets and schoolrooms.

Inside, the music changed. A faster beat. A familiar tune.

Jackie gasped. "Oh! That's my song!"

She tugged Barry's arm. "Come on, slowcoach, let's get in there!"

"Oi," Barry said, but he let himself be dragged.

The others followed in a warm, jostling cluster—Kevin and June, Brian and Maureen, Martin weaving between them making snide comments about Barry's dancing, Tony guiding Maggie with a hand on her back, Brenda holding Dougie's arm as if anchoring him to the moment.

Dougie paused at the doorway, taking it in—the swirling lights, the laughter, the music alive with promise. For one fleeting second he wondered how many more nights like this they'd have. How many more times all of them would be here, together, unchanged. Brenda squeezed his hand. "You coming?"

"Yeah," he said, stepping inside. "I'm coming."

The door swung shut behind them, swallowing the river light, and the night began.

The moment the group stepped into The Riverview, the air wrapped around them—thick with cigarette smoke, perfume, hair spray, and the unmistakable scent of sweat from bodies that had been moving for hours. The lights were low, coloured bulbs casting pinks and blues over the dance floor. Up on the small wooden stage, a local band hammered out a beat that thrummed right through your chest.

Jackie pulled Barry straight into the wave of dancers, already moving before they found space.

"Slow down!" Barry laughed, trying to keep up with her rhythm.

"Don't slow down, speed up!" she shouted back, throwing her head back with delight.

Maggie and Tony drifted towards the bar, hands intertwined. Tony ordered drinks—two lemonades—and looked around with the calm confidence of someone who'd been coming

THE MEDWAY YEARS

here long enough to be recognised. Maggie sipped her drink and leaned against him, though her eyes roamed the room in a way Tony didn't quite catch.

Martin Prentice was already in rare form, sliding across the polished floor in exaggerated dance steps, earning laughs from strangers and groans from his friends.

"If he falls on his backside," Kevin muttered to Dougie, "I'm not helping him up."

"You say that every week," Dougie said.

"Yeah, but this time I mean it."

Kevin scanned the hall for June, who had drifted toward a group of girls from work. He tried waving, but she didn't see him.

"Go on," Dougie nudged. "Go talk to her."

"In a minute," Kevin said, though he didn't move. "Want to see if Brian gets himself in trouble first."

Brian was already halfway there. He had that easy, natural charm that didn't try too hard—and somehow tried too hard at the same time. As he crossed the dance floor, several girls glanced at him, and he smiled politely back. Maureen saw each look, each smile, and her lips tightened just enough for Dougie to notice.

"Do you want a drink?" Maureen asked Brian.

"I'll grab one in a bit," Brian said vaguely, eyes drifting toward the dancers.

THE MEDWAY YEARS

Maureen inhaled slowly. "Right."

Dougie turned to Brenda. "Drink?"

She nodded, and he guided her toward the bar, weaving between couples and groups talking loudly over the music.

Brenda leaned close to be heard. "Do you think Tony's all right?"

Dougie glanced over at Tony, who had his arm around Maggie but was scanning the room with a faint crease in his brow.
"Seems fine."

"He seems… tense tonight."

"Maybe he's just tired."

"Or maybe he thinks someone's after Maggie," Brenda said with a knowing tilt of her head.

Dougie shrugged, but she wasn't wrong. Tony had a habit of keeping one eye on Maggie wherever she went, and tonight his grip on her hand had been a touch too firm.

At the bar, the barman—an older fellow with rolled-up sleeves and a thinning moustache—nodded at them. "What'll it be?"

Before Dougie could answer, a voice piped up behind him. "Two pints, one lemonade, and a packet of crisps, barkeep. Put it on Dougie's tab."

Martin slid in between them, grinning broadly.

"Don't mind him," Dougie said. "He thinks he's funny."

THE MEDWAY YEARS

"I *am* funny," Martin insisted. "Ask anyone."

"Anyone sober," Brenda muttered.

Martin clutched his chest in mock injury. "Cruel. Truly cruel."

The drinks arrived, and for a moment the three of them stood watching the dance floor. The band had shifted into a slower number, and Barry now held Jackie with a gentleness that surprised anyone who thought they knew him. Her head rested on his shoulder, eyes closed, content.

"They're good together," Brenda said softly.

"Too good," Martin sniffed. "Makes the rest of us look bad."

Dougie glanced at the others. Tony had his hands on Maggie's waist, guiding her in tiny, precise steps. Brian danced with Maureen, though he seemed distracted, glancing over her shoulder at the stage. Kevin had finally approached June and now stood uncertainly by her side, trying to look confident and failing charmingly.

Dougie sipped his drink. "Looks like everyone's doing all right."

Brenda turned to him. "And us?"

He looked at her—really looked this time. She had dressed up tonight: hair neat, bright lipstick, a blouse she'd said was "nothing special," though it clearly mattered to her. She was trying. She always tried. "We're good," he said quietly.

Her smile was small but sincere.

THE MEDWAY YEARS

The music shifted again, picking up pace. The dance floor exploded back to life. "Come on," Brenda urged. "I want a turn before Martin embarrasses us all."

"Too late for that," Martin said, already heading back into the chaos.

Dougie took her hand, and they stepped onto the floor. The music pulsed around them, the crowd warm and alive. For a few minutes, everything seemed easy—simpler than real life, simpler than work or money or uncertain futures.

But as Dougie spun Brenda beneath the coloured lights, he caught sight of his friends scattered across the hall— laughing, dancing, pretending they weren't worried about anything—and wondered how many of these moments would last.

People change. Lives shift. Love doesn't always stay where you leave it.

But not tonight. Tonight, the Riverview held them all together. For now.

CHAPTER TWO – The Morning After

Sunday mornings in Medway always felt slower than the rest of the week, as if the whole town were nursing the same mild hangover. Church bells drifted over rooftops, milk floats rattled along quiet streets, and the scent of coal fires mixed with the cool river breeze. It was a day for families, fry-ups, and pretending you weren't out too late the night before.

THE MEDWAY YEARS

Dougie woke to the muffled sound of his mum clattering pans downstairs. His head wasn't pounding, but it wasn't exactly clear either. He lay for a moment, staring at the ceiling, replaying bits of last night—the lights, the music, Brenda's laughter, the odd way Tony kept glancing around the room as if expecting trouble.

He dragged himself out of bed and made his way downstairs, shirt half-buttoned.

"Morning, love," his mum said without turning from the cooker. "Breakfast will be ready in a minute. You lot had a fun time?"

"Not bad."

"Not bad?" she repeated, giving him a sharp look. "You come home humming and smiling like a fool, and that's 'not bad'?"

He grinned. "All right, we had a good time."

"Thought so. Your Brenda's a nice girl. Reliable. You could do a lot worse."

Dougie knew this speech. He'd heard it often enough. "Yes, Mum."

"Don't 'yes Mum' me. You listen. Girls like her don't come around twice."

He sat down at the table and picked at the edge of the newspaper. He wasn't going to argue. Not because she was right or wrong, but because he didn't know what he felt yet, not really.

THE MEDWAY YEARS

His mum slid a plate in front of him. "Eat. Then go see her. She'll be expecting it."

He nodded, though he wasn't sure he'd go.

Across town, Tony Marks was washing his father's car with more force than necessary. The water sloshed violently over the bonnet, soaking his shoes.

His father stepped out of the house. "You all right, boy?"

"I'm fine."

"You look like you're trying to drown my poor motor."

Tony didn't smile. He kept scrubbing. He'd barely slept. Something about last night gnawed at him. Maggie had been radiant, glowing in her dress, drawing looks from half the hall. It shouldn't have bothered him—she'd chosen him, hadn't she?—but the idea of losing her made something inside him tighten.

His father sighed. "If you start a day angry, it's hard to end it any different."

"I'm not angry." But he was. At what, he didn't know.

Meanwhile, Maggie lay in bed, staring at the ceiling in her family's small terrace home. She replayed the dance in her mind—not Tony's hand arm around her waist, but the laughter of her friends, the warmth of the music, the feeling of being alive and free. She loved Tony, she did, but sometimes his protectiveness felt like a coat she hadn't asked to wear.

THE MEDWAY YEARS

Her mother knocked. "You getting up today?"

"In a minute."

"Don't waste the sunshine, love."

Maggie smiled faintly. Sunshine. Maybe she needed some of that.

Barry Medhurst woke to the sound of the neighbour's radio blaring. He groaned, rubbing his eyes. Jackie had danced him to exhaustion last night. He could still feel the ache in his legs.

He glanced out the window. Sure enough, Jackie was already outside, standing on the pavement in a bright yellow dress, waving up at his window.

He leaned out. "What are you doing here this early?"

"It's nearly ten!"

"That's early."

"Come on," she called. "Walk with me. I want some fresh air."

Barry couldn't deny her anything, not really. "Give me five minutes."

As he got dressed, he wondered how long he could keep up with her energy. Jackie was full of fire—fun, laughter, life. Sometimes he felt like she deserved someone flashier, someone who could match her spark. But she chose him. And that counted for something.

THE MEDWAY YEARS

Brian Batchelor woke on his back, staring at the cracks in the ceiling of his small room. His head throbbed. Not from drink—he hadn't had that much—but from thinking too much.

He'd enjoyed last night. Maybe too much. He remembered dancing with Maureen, but also the eyes of other girls catching his. He didn't do anything wrong—not really—but he knew Maureen had noticed. She always noticed.

Downstairs, Maureen sat at her kitchen table, stirring tea she wasn't drinking. Her mother moved around the room, humming softly.

"You're quiet today," her mum said.

"Just tired."

Her mother gave her a knowing look. "That boy of yours treating you right?"

"Yes," Maureen said automatically.

But something inside her twisted. Loving Brian always felt like holding something that wanted to be free.

Kevin Powers was already out in the street, kicking a football against a brick wall. *Thud. Catch. Turn. Kick.*

He practiced every day, Sunday or not. Sweat beaded on his forehead even in the morning cool.

June watched him from her window, chin resting on her hand. He hadn't knocked for her. Again.

THE MEDWAY YEARS

She wasn't angry—not exactly—but a heaviness sat in her chest. She wanted to be supportive. She wanted to believe in his dream. But watching him chase the same ball every morning while she sat alone in her room made her feel like a footnote in his life.

Her mother passed the doorway. "He's out there again?"

"Yes."

"Football's all well and good," her mother said gently, "but a girl can't wait forever." June didn't answer.

Martin Prentice woke on the sofa, still wearing half the clothes from last night. His father must've fallen asleep in the armchair again, empty bottles cluttering the floor.

Martin slipped out quietly, not wanting to wake him. He walked the streets alone, hands shoved in his pockets, whistling a tune from the dance. He tried to shake off the cold feeling that always crept in after a good night—the reminder that laughter didn't fix everything, not when home still felt like a place you escaped from rather than returned to.

He headed toward the park, needing fresh air, space, anything that wasn't four walls and silence.

After breakfast, Dougie wandered the streets aimlessly. The town felt different in daylight—less magical than the night before, more real. Kids played in front gardens. Men washed cars. Women hung laundry. Churchgoers strolled in neat lines towards the chapel.

Dougie wasn't sure where he was going until he found himself standing outside Barry's house, just as Barry stepped out with Jackie.

"All right?" Barry called.

"Fancy a walk?" Jackie asked, bright as ever.

Dougie shrugged. "Why not."

As they walked together, Dougie realised something. Nights like The Riverview were the easy part. Anyone could feel happy under coloured lights and loud music.

But mornings—quiet, honest mornings—were where people's real lives lived. And today, each of them was waking to a truth they might not want to face. Something was shifting.
He could feel it.

DOWN BY THE MEDWAY

The river always drew people on a Sunday. Families picnicked along the grassy banks, children dangled fishing lines that never caught anything, and couples strolled lazily, enjoying the rare warmth the English sun bothered to offer.

Dougie, Barry, and Jackie arrived first. Jackie had insisted they walk "somewhere with sky," and Barry, hopelessly loyal to her whims, agreed without question. Dougie followed, kicking stones half-heartedly along the path.

THE MEDWAY YEARS

Jackie spread out a small blanket and flopped onto it immediately. "Oh, this is perfect," she sighed. "I could live right here."

Barry snorted. "You'd last ten minutes before complaining about ants." "Probably," she admitted, smiling.

Dougie sat on the grass beside them, leaning back on his hands, letting the sunlight warm his face. Across the water, a pair of rowboats drifted slow and steady, oars dipping rhythmically. The river shimmered—grey, but somehow beautiful.

"Thought Brenda might be here," Jackie said casually.

Dougie shrugged. "Haven't seen her today."

Jackie gave Barry a pointed look, but he wisely stayed silent.

They sat in comfortable quiet until footsteps approached. Kevin Powers appeared first, football under his arm, June trailing behind. She gave a small wave.

"Fancy seeing you lot," Kevin said, though it was clear he'd hoped for an audience.

"You been playing all morning?" Barry asked.

Kevin grinned. "Course. Got to keep sharp."

June lowered herself onto the grass a little distance from the blanket. "He didn't even stop for lunch."

"You could've eaten without me," Kevin said lightly.

But June didn't answer. She just tucked her skirt under her legs and watched the river.

THE MEDWAY YEARS

A moment later, Martin Prentice arrived, hands deep in his pockets, kicking at imaginary objects as he walked. He dropped onto the grass with an exaggerated groan.

"What happened to you?" Dougie asked.

"Life," Martin said dramatically. "It's exhausting. I need a holiday."

"You need a job," Barry muttered.

Martin grinned. "That too."

It wasn't long before two more figures appeared on the path—Maggie and Brian walking side by side. They weren't talking, not exactly, but Maggie was laughing at something Brian had said, and his grin was unmistakable.

Barry raised an eyebrow. Dougie sat forward.

Behind them, several paces back, came Maureen. Her careful posture and clipped steps told the whole story.

Maggie spotted the group first. "Oh! Look who's here!"

Brian lifted a hand. "Afternoon."

Maureen remained silent as she joined them, but the tension wrapped around her like a thin coat.

Tony arrived moments later from the opposite direction, jogging slightly as if he'd hurried once he saw the group gathered. His eyes went straight to Maggie, then to Brian, then back to Maggie.

"Didn't know you were coming out," Tony said, a forced brightness in his voice.

THE MEDWAY YEARS

Maggie smiled up at him. "Just fancied a walk."

"With me," Brian added, perhaps unintentionally.

Tony's jaw tightened. Dougie felt Barry shift slightly beside him.

Martin, sensing the drop in air pressure, clapped loudly. "Well! What a beautiful day for tension! Who's got sandwiches?"

Jackie threw a small pebble at him. "Honestly, Martin."

But the moment was diffused—barely.

They formed a wider circle on the grass, some sitting, some standing. Conversation started awkwardly, threads crossing over each other without settling.

Kevin bounced the football off his knee. Maggie watched the river. Maureen watched Maggie. Tony watched Brian.

Brian watched nothing in particular, pretending all was fine.

Dougie saw everything. He always did.

"So," Martin said loudly, desperate to stir life back into the group, "does anyone want to see me fall in the river?"

"No!" June said immediately. "Yes," Kevin said at the same time.

Martin stood up dramatically, marched to the water's edge, wobbled his arms comically—and stopped just short of falling in.

THE MEDWAY YEARS

Jackie laughed—really laughed—and Barry couldn't help smiling. Even Maggie and Maureen cracked small smiles. It was enough. Just enough to lighten the moment.

Kevin tossed the football toward Barry. "Kickabout?"

Barry nodded and stood. "Dougie, you in?"

"Yeah," Dougie said, rising to his feet.

Kevin gestured at Brian. "Come on, big man. Let's see if you can aim as well as you can dance."

Brian grinned, accepting the challenge, and jogged over. Tony hesitated, calculating, then followed. It felt safer to be part of the game than to let Brian and Maggie share another private laugh.

The impromptu match quickly turned chaotic—feet sliding in the grass, Martin shouting fictional rules, Jackie cheering loudly for both sides. Even June found herself smiling despite her earlier mood.

On the sideline, Maggie leaned toward Maureen. "Sorry I didn't wait for you earlier. Brian just… walked with me."

Maureen stared at the boys playing. "He walks with whoever's beside him."

Maggie sighed. "He didn't mean anything by it."

"I know," Maureen said. "But understanding something doesn't always make it easy."

Maggie opened her mouth to reply, but the sound of laughter pulled her attention back to the match. Tony had tripped over

22

THE MEDWAY YEARS

Martin, sending them both tumbling. Even Tony laughed—though there was an edge to it.

"Idiots," Maggie said fondly. Maureen smiled. "All of them."

As the boys kept playing, wildly and with little skill, Dougie paused for breath. He looked around—the river glittering behind them, the group scattered across the bank in sunlight and laughter—and felt a pang of something he couldn't name.

These were the good days. He knew it even then. But good days didn't last forever. People drift. People change. And sometimes all it takes is one Sunday afternoon to start the shift.

THE MEDWAY YEARS

CHAPTER THREE – Enter Mike Weston

The weeks after that Sunday at the riverbank passed quietly enough on the surface, but for Tony and Maggie, something had shifted—something subtle, like a floorboard beginning to creak long before it snaps.

Maggie felt it first.

Maggie worked in the office of a small furniture showroom on the High Street, answering phones, typing invoices, and filing order forms for customers who wanted new sideboards or wardrobes on instalment plans. The job wasn't thrilling, but it gave her a sense of independence Tony didn't quite understand.

Mike Weston walked in on a Wednesday morning.

He was older than Tony—mid-twenties, confident in that casual, effortless way of men who've seen a bit more of the world. Dark suit, polished shoes, tie slightly loosened, hair neatly combed. He carried a sample case in one hand and a smile in the other.

"Morning," he said, tipping his head toward her desk. "Is your manager in?"

"He is," Maggie said. "I'll let him know you're here."

THE MEDWAY YEARS

But Mike lingered.

"You're new," he said lightly. "Haven't seen you before."

"I started a few months ago."

"Well," he said, "the place has improved since my last visit."

Maggie felt a warmth rise in her cheeks—an unexpected, unfamiliar warmth. "Don't say things like that," she said, trying to sound stern.

He only smiled wider. "It's not flattery if it's true."

She tried to focus on her typing afterward, but she could feel his presence in the manager's office across the room—the low murmur of his voice, the occasional glance he threw her way. When he left, he tipped his head again as he passed.

"See you next time, Miss…?"

"Heston."

"Miss Heston," he repeated, savouring it. "Take care."

Maggie tried to shake off the feeling he left behind—light, airy, dangerous.

TONY'S GROWING UNEASE

Tony noticed the change before Maggie realised it was visible.

She laughed more at trivial things. She spent longer on her hair before going out. She seemed distracted sometimes, lost in thoughts she didn't share.

THE MEDWAY YEARS

One evening outside The Riverview, Tony caught her looking down the street, as if expecting someone.

"Waiting for somebody?" he asked casually.

She blinked. "What? No. Don't be silly."

But she didn't meet his eyes.

Inside the hall, Maggie danced with her friends but seemed far away. Tony watched her closely—too closely.

When Brian chatted to her near the bar, Tony inserted himself between them within seconds.

When she stepped outside for fresh air, he followed.

"Tony," she sighed, "you don't have to watch me all night."

"I'm not watching," he said stiffly. "I'm just with you."

But his grip on her arm told another story.

GROWING CONNECTION

Mike Weston returned to the shop the next week. Then again the week after.

Sometimes he had order forms. Sometimes he had nothing but a charming excuse.

"Passing by," he'd say with a wink. "Thought I'd brighten the place."

They chatted at her desk in brief, stolen minutes—about music, London, the places he travelled for work.

THE MEDWAY YEARS

"Ever been to London for a night out?" he asked one morning.

"No," Maggie admitted. "Tony doesn't really like… big places."

"Shame," Mike said. "A city like that? You'd light it up."

She laughed nervously. "You don't even know me."

"Oh, I do," Mike said gently. "Better than you think."

Maggie felt something dangerous flutter in her chest.

TONY'S CONTROL SLIPS

One Friday evening, Tony suggested they skip the dance.

"Let's stay in," he said. "Just the two of us."

"I promised Jackie I'd be there," Maggie replied.

"I'd rather you stayed with me."

She hesitated, something inside her tightening. "Tony… you can't decide where I go."

His jaw flexed. "I'm not deciding. I'm asking."

"No," Maggie said softly. "You're telling."

That moment—small but piercing—hung between them.

At the dance, Tony barely left her side. When she laughed with Martin, Tony pulled her away. When she went to the ladies' room, he stood outside waiting. When Brian said a simple hello, Tony's eyes flashed.

27

THE MEDWAY YEARS

Maggie felt suffocated. For the first time, she wondered if the life ahead of her with Tony would be small. Too small for the dreams she barely dared acknowledge.

THE SECRET MEETING

The next Tuesday, on her lunch break, she saw Mike across the street loading his samples into his car.

He waved. She waved back.

He nodded toward the café on the corner. She hesitated——then crossed the road.

They talked for twenty minutes. Then thirty.

Mike asked gently, "Are you happy, Maggie?"

She opened her mouth to say yes. The word didn't come.

He didn't push further. He simply said, "You deserve a life that fits you."

When she returned to work, her hands trembled on the typewriter keys.

THE BREAKDOWN

The following Saturday night was the one that broke them.

They were walking home from the dance, the streets damp from an earlier drizzle, the lamps casting long shadows. Maggie's mind was miles away—thinking of Mike, of London, of possibilities.

THE MEDWAY YEARS

Tony sensed it. "Where are you tonight?" he asked quietly.

"I don't know," she said. "Just tired."

"You're different lately."

"Am I?"

"Yes. And I don't like it."

She stopped walking. The words landed hard.

"Well," she said, voice trembling, "maybe that's the problem."

Tony stared. "What's that supposed to mean?"

"It means I can't breathe, Tony." She wiped her eyes quickly. "I can't move without you checking where I'm going."

"I'm just looking out for you."

"No," she whispered. "You're holding on too tight."

He reached for her. She stepped back. That tiny movement did more damage than any argument.

"Maggie... don't do this."

"I have to." She said

THE DECISION

Two days later, she met Mike again—this time deliberately.

THE MEDWAY YEARS

He sat beside her on a bench overlooking the river.

"You all right?" he asked softly.

"No," she said truthfully. "But I will be."

He nodded as if he understood exactly what she meant.

"I've had an offer," Mike said. "A position in London. Good money, lots of travel. I'm heading there next Monday."

Maggie swallowed. A choice hovered in the air, unspoken but bright as a spark.

"I need to leave Medway," she whispered. "I need… something else."

Mike looked at her carefully—not pushing, not assuming. "Then come," he said quietly. "Only if *you* want to."

Maggie closed her eyes.

She saw Tony's anger, his fear, his love that felt like a cage. And she saw London—lights, movement, independence, possibility.

She opened her eyes. "I'm coming."

THE FINAL BREAK

THE MEDWAY YEARS

Tony came to her house the next evening, unaware of any of it yet. His face brightened when she answered the door. "Maggie… look, about the other night—"

"I'm leaving," she said softly.

His breath caught. "Leaving what?"

"Medway."

It was as if she'd punched him. "What are you talking about?"

"I'm going to London."

"With whom?" His voice was already cracking.

She didn't lie. "Mike Weston."

The world seemed to fall out from under Tony's feet.

"You've been seeing him?" His voice rose. "Behind my back?"

"Not like that," she whispered. "I just… talked to him. And I realised things I couldn't with you."

Tony stared at her—as if she had shattered something inside him he didn't know was fragile.

"You said you loved me."

"I did," Maggie said. "I still do in a way. But not… not enough to stay."

Tony stepped back as if struck. "You're making a mistake."

"Maybe," she said. "But it's mine to make."

THE MEDWAY YEARS

She closed the door softly. Tony stood outside until the streetlamps flickered out.

CHAPTER FOUR – The Fall of Tony Marks

The night Maggie left Medway, something in Tony Marks broke—clean through, like a plank cracked under too much weight. He walked home slowly, numb to the cold, numb to the drizzle that blurred the streetlamps, numb to everything except the echo of Maggie's words:

"I'm going to London." "With Mike." "It's my choice."

He replayed them until they carved grooves into his mind.

SILENCE AT HOME

His parents were still awake when he came in. His mother rose from her chair the moment she saw his face. "Tony? What's wrong?"

He didn't answer. He went straight to his bedroom, shut the door quietly, then slid down against it until he was sitting on the floor. His mother tried knocking, asked gently what had happened, but he said nothing.

Eventually, she gave up.

Tony stayed awake the entire night, staring at the pattern of the wallpaper until dawn.

THE FIRST DRINK

He didn't go to work the next day. Or the one after that.

THE MEDWAY YEARS

His foreman gave him the benefit of the doubt—Tony had always been dependable. But by the third day of absence, the warnings began. Tony ignored them.

Instead, he wandered the streets of Medway, hands in his pockets, shoulders hunched, eyes vacant. People greeted him—older neighbours, blokes from the yard—but he barely heard them.

On the fourth morning, he walked into *The King's Arms*, a pub he'd only ever gone to for celebrations.

The landlord raised his eyebrows. "All right, Tony? You look done in."

Tony nodded stiffly. "Whisky."

"On a Tuesday morning?" the landlord muttered, but poured it anyway.

Tony drank it in one go. It burned, but at least it made him feel *something*. He ordered another. And another.

By the time he left, the sky was darkening with rainclouds, and his steps were uneven.

It became a new routine. A dangerous one.

FRIENDS START TO NOTICE

Barry was the first to see him stumbling near the High Street one evening. "Tony! Mate—bloody hell—are you all right?"

THE MEDWAY YEARS

Tony swayed, tried to focus. "Get off me."

"I'm not on you," Barry said calmly. "What's going on?"

Tony shoved him. "Leave me alone, Barry."

Barry caught himself, stunned. Tony had never shoved anyone in his life.

"Look," Barry said gently, "I heard about Maggie, but this isn't the way-out mate."

Tony's voice exploded, sharp and pained. "Don't say her name!"

Barry stepped back, hands raised. "All right. All right."

Tony walked off, weaving down the pavement like a man trying to outrun his own shadow.

THE JOB GOES

At work, things deteriorated fast. Tony arrived late—if he arrived at all. He snapped at co-workers. He made mistakes with measurements, something he'd never done before. He showed up more than once smelling clearly of drink.

The foreman pulled him aside.

"Tony, lad… you're not right. Talk to me."

"I'm fine."

"You're not. This isn't you."

Tony stared at the floor.

THE MEDWAY YEARS

"We'll give you another chance," the foreman said. "But one more slip, and I'll have no choice."

Two days later, Tony didn't show up at all. That was it. The dismissal letter came a week later.

His father held it in his hands, angry but more heartbroken than anything. "What happened to you, son?" Tony didn't answer.
He just took the letter and left the house.

THE GROUP STEPS BACK

At first, the others tried to help.

Dougie approached him near Chatham station. "Tony, come on. Talk to us. Let us help."

Tony glared at him. "You? Help? You couldn't help yourself if you tried."

It was a cruel blow—unexpected and sharp. Dougie stepped back, stung.

Brenda whispered to him later, "He's hurting. Truly hurting."

"I know," Dougie murmured. "But he's not letting anyone near."

Brian tried too, approaching Tony outside a pub. "Fancy a chat?"

Tony's eyes darkened. "You think I don't know you always fancied her?"

THE MEDWAY YEARS

Brian froze. "Tony, that's not—"

"Go on," Tony spat. "Say it. You were waiting your turn."

Brian shook his head. "You're not well, mate."

"Get away from me!" Tony shouted, loud enough that passers-by stared.

Brian backed off. It was the first time he'd ever been afraid of Tony.

Eventually, the group stopped trying. Not because they didn't care—because every attempt ended in hostility.

Maureen summed it up one evening: "He wants to fall. We can't stop him until he stops himself."

No one disagreed.

SLIPPING THROUGH THE CRACKS

Tony's parents tried to hold him up—meals, stern talks, gentle talks, threats, pleas—but he stopped coming home. He drifted in and out of pubs, slept on benches near the river or in alleys behind the High Street.

He looked different now—unshaven, clothes creased, eyes hollow. Even the landlord at The King's Arms refused to serve him at times.

"Go home, lad," he'd say. "You're scaring the customers."

Tony would just stare, then walk out into the night with his hands trembling.

THE MEDWAY YEARS

Weeks turned into months. People whispered about him—
*That Marks boy, shame really, handsome lad, too,
heartbreak will do that.*

He became a shadow moving through Medway.

A MAN IN A DOORWAY

One cold evening in November, Dougie and Barry walked
past the Co-op on the High Street. A figure was huddled in
the doorway, knees drawn to his chest, coat pulled tight.

Barry slowed. "Is that—?"

It was Tony. He looked up at them with red, unfocused eyes.

"Got any change?" he slurred.

Dougie exhaled, heart sinking. "Tony… it's us."

Tony shrugged. "I know who you are."

"Come on," Barry said. "Let's get you somewhere warm."

"No." Tony's voice was flat. "I'm fine here."

"You're not."

Tony snapped suddenly, eyes blazing. "Leave me alone.
Both of you. Just go."

It wasn't the words that hit hardest—it was the emptiness
behind them. Not anger. Not defiance. Just surrender.

Barry swallowed hard. Dougie's chest tightened.

THE MEDWAY YEARS

They stepped away because there was nothing left to say—and because Tony no longer wanted saving.

Behind them, Tony slumped back into the doorway, the night swallowing him whole.

A CHANGED MAN

By winter, the Tony Marks they once knew was gone.

In his place was a man who barely spoke, barely smiled, barely existed. His sharp suits long gone. His confidence dissolved.
His future collapsed. He drifted from doorway to doorway, bottle to bottle, day to day.

Maggie's name was hardly ever spoken among the group anymore. Not out of anger—out of grief.

Dougie said it best one night, sitting with Barry by the riverbank:

"It's not just that he lost her," Dougie said quietly. "It's that he lost himself."

Barry nodded. "Question is… will he ever find his way back?"

The river flowed on, silent and indifferent. And Tony Marks, once the brightest of them, remained lost in the shadows.

THE MEDWAY YEARS

CHAPTER FIVE – The Offer on the Touchline

Sunday league football always drew a crowd in Medway, even when the wind cut like a knife and the pitch was more mud than grass. The lads played for pride mostly, though Kevin Powers played like something more was on the line— every match, every minute.

It was late autumn now, the trees bare, the sky a dull iron grey. The field in Rochester was wet from a morning drizzle,

THE MEDWAY YEARS

puddles glinting between the divots. Still, Kevin laced his boots with the same fierce determination he always had.

June stood near the touchline, hands tucked inside her coat sleeves, cheeks pink from the cold. She didn't love football, not really, but she loved Kevin—enough to watch him run himself ragged every Sunday.

Barry and Dougie were there too, stamping their feet to stay warm.

"Reckon he'll score today?" Dougie asked.

"Course he will," Barry replied. "He's been itching for it all week."

June offered a small smile. "He always plays better when there's someone to impress."

"Meaning you," Barry said kindly.

She didn't answer, only looked back at Kevin—her Kevin—bouncing on the balls of his feet, eyes scanning the pitch like a general reading a battlefield.

THE MATCH BEGINS

The whistle blew.

Kevin sprang forward immediately, covering the pitch with a speed that shocked the opposing side. He wasn't the biggest lad, not the strongest either, but he had a rare agility—quick turns, sharp instincts, and the ability to slip through gaps others didn't even see.

THE MEDWAY YEARS

June watched him with a mixture of pride and worry. He lived for this. Sometimes she feared he lived *only* for this.

The crowd murmured with approval as Kevin darted down the left wing, flicked the ball past a defender, and cut inside. A shot—low, powerful, precise—forced the keeper to stretch fully to tip it away.

Dougie whistled. "Close one."

"He's on form today," Barry said. "Properly on form."

But someone else had noticed too.

A man in a long dark coat stood apart from the crowd, hands behind his back, eyes never leaving Kevin. Middle-aged, neat haircut, scarf in Gillingham blue. He watched with a calm intensity that made June uneasy without knowing why.

Kevin Shines

Before long, Kevin got what he was hunting.

Midway through the second half, Barry's cousin—the team's lanky midfielder—sent a high ball arcing forward. Kevin sprinted, overtook the full-back, let the ball drop, then struck it on the half-volley. Straight into the net.

The crowd erupted. Kevin punched the air, grinning wildly, his teammates swarming him.

June felt her heart swell—then twist, just a little. Moments like this always filled her with both love and fear.

As the players jogged back to their positions, the man in the dark coat nodded once, as if confirming something.

41

THE MEDWAY YEARS

The match ended 2–1, with Kevin's goal the difference. The lads shook hands, clapped each other on the back, and trudged off the muddy pitch toward the scattered spectators.

Kevin spotted June first. His grin was unstoppable.

"Did you see it?" he said breathlessly. "Of course I did," she said. "It was brilliant."

Then the man in the coat stepped forward. "Kevin Powers?" he asked.

Kevin blinked. "Yeah?"

The man extended a hand. "Name's **Geoff Turner**. I'm with **Gillingham Football Club**."

Barry's eyebrows shot up. Dougie nearly choked on his breath.

Kevin froze. "You're… with Gillingham?"

"That's right. I oversee youth recruitment and trial sessions. Been watching you today—and last Sunday as well."

June's stomach dropped. *Last Sunday?* She hadn't even known the man was there.

Kevin swallowed hard. "I—well—thank you. Sir."

Turner smiled. "You've got pace, lad. And an eye for goal. Raw, yes. Rough around the edges. But there's something there."

THE MEDWAY YEARS

Kevin's heart hammered against his ribs. June felt her breath thinning.

Turner continued, "We're looking to bring in a few promising local lads for **trial training**. See what they can do on a bigger pitch, under proper coaching."

Kevin stared, barely able to speak. "Are you… offering me a trial?"

Turner nodded. " If you can report to the Gillingham training ground next Tuesday at five, boots, kit, the works, we'll see if you can handle it."

Kevin let out a shaky laugh, somewhere between disbelief and joy. "Yes. Yes—of course. I'll be there."

Turner gave him a firm handshake. "Good lad. Don't be late."

He walked off down the path, leaving a stunned silence in his wake.

THE REACTIONS

Barry was the first to react. "Kevin, you bloody superstar!"

Dougie slapped Kevin's back. "This is massive!"

Kevin laughed, breathless. "I can't believe it… I can't."

June smiled, but it was tight around the edges. "That's wonderful, Kevin."

He turned to her, eyes alight with pride and something bigger—ambition, even destiny.

THE MEDWAY YEARS

"June, this is it," he said urgently. "This is what I've been waiting for."

"I know," she said softly. "I know it means everything to you."

"It does," Kevin said. "It really does."

He looked back toward where the scout had gone, eyes shining, mind already racing ahead to Tuesday, to the training ground, to the dream he'd carried since he was a boy.

June watched him—really watched him—and felt a cold truth settle in her heart:

If football chose Kevin, she might lose what little space she had left in his life.

But she wouldn't say it. Not today. Not when he was standing on the edge of everything he'd ever wanted.

Kevin turned to her again, grabbed her hands, grinning like the world had cracked open for him.

"June, you're coming with me Tuesday, right? You'll be there?"

She hesitated a fraction of a second too long. "Of course," she said finally, forcing the warmth back into her smile.

Kevin didn't notice the hesitation. He didn't notice much of anything except the future rushing toward him.

As they walked away from the pitch, Kevin animatedly describing how he'd impress the coaches, June walked beside him in silence—proud, supportive… and quietly terrified.

CHAPTER SIX– "Trials and Fault Lines"

The Gillingham training ground sat behind a tall chain-link fence, the kind that rattled in the wind and made everything inside feel more important. Floodlights towered above the pitch like silent guardians. Even though it was only late afternoon, the sky was dim, winter creeping closer with every breath of chilly air.

Kevin stood at the gate, kit bag slung over his shoulder, heart pounding so loudly he thought June might hear it. June stood beside him, her gloved hands gripping each other tightly.

"You'll do brilliant," she said.

He nodded but didn't speak. His mouth was too dry.

THE MEDWAY YEARS

A whistle shrilled inside the ground, echoing faintly.

"Right," he whispered. "Let's go."

June smiled, - small, nervous, proud, and followed him toward the entrance, where a surly-looking assistant checked names off a clipboard.

"Powers?"
"Yes, sir."

"Boots clean?"

"Yes."

 "Good. First impressions matter here."

Kevin gulped.

June watched him step onto the gravel path leading toward the training pitch as if he were walking into a different world.

Because he was.

FIRST STEPS ON THE PITCH

A group of lads were already warming up—fifteen, maybe twenty of them—stretching, jogging, showing off little bursts of skill when they thought the coaches weren't looking.

Most were bigger than Kevin. Some looked older. One lad in a Gillingham tracksuit whispered to another, eyes flicking to Kevin with a smirk.

Kevin felt small. Light. Too thin. Too... ordinary.

THE MEDWAY YEARS

A coach in a thick navy jacket strode toward him. "You Powers?"

"Yes, sir."

"Turner says you've got pace. We'll see. Warm up."

And that was that.

No welcome speech. No hand on the shoulder. Just pressure.

Kevin jogged over to the others, stretching, trying to loosen his legs. His stomach churned like waves on the riverbank.

June watched from behind the fence, breath misting in the cold, fingers gripping the wire. She had never seen Kevin look intimidated. It scared her.

INTENSITY & COMPETITION

The drills started immediately.

Short sprints. Possession circles. One-touch passing. Tight-angled shooting.

Kevin struggled early. His passes were rushed. His first sprint was only middle of the pack. Twice the ball slipped under his foot.

He heard laughter from somewhere behind him, followed by a muttered, "Kent lads always think they're quicker than they are."

Kevin flushed hot, shame burning his ears.

THE MEDWAY YEARS

June winced from the fence. She hated seeing him falter. She hated even more that she couldn't reach him.

But then— Something changed.

Kevin's breathing steadied. His touch smoothed out. He found the rhythm of the drills.

And when the coach shouted for the **acceleration test**, Kevin came alive.

A line of cones stretched across the pitch. Each lad had to sprint, turn, sprint again.

Kevin exploded forward like a spark catching dry tinder.

He wasn't just fast— he was *fluid*, *fearless*, cutting angles like the ground itself bent to his will.

He finished first. By a distance.

One of the coaches murmured, "There it is."

Another nodded. "Raw, but that's pace you can't teach."

Kevin caught June's eye across the fence. She beamed. He beamed back. For a moment, everything was perfect.

SCRIMMAGE – THE REAL TEST

The lads were split into two teams for a final scrimmage. Blue bibs versus red.

Kevin was given blue.

The whistle blew.

THE MEDWAY YEARS

The ball zipped across the pitch. Bodies collided. Shouts filled the air. It was faster, harder, more demanding than anything Kevin had played in before. But he didn't shrink.

He rose. He chased everything—lost causes, wild passes, impossible angles.

"Use your pace, Powers!" a coach yelled.

Kevin did.

He darted past defenders, sprinting onto a through-ball. A centre-back tried to shoulder him off, but Kevin stayed tall, driving forward.

He struck. Hard. The keeper saved, but only just.

The coaches exchanged a look.

"Promising," one said.

"Very," said another.

But not everyone approved.

A tall, broad lad—clearly the local favourite—cut across Kevin after the play.

"Don't think you're special," he muttered. "One fast run doesn't make you first-team material."

Kevin stared him down, refusing to be cowed. But the seed of intimidation had been planted.

JUNE'S INSECURITY GROWS

THE MEDWAY YEARS

June watched the entire session, the cold numbing her fingers, her toes, her thoughts. She saw Kevin shine. She also saw how badly he wanted this. Too badly.

When the scrimmage paused for water, Kevin didn't jog over to her. He didn't wave. He didn't even look for her.

He stood with the lads instead, listening to the coaches, soaking up every word.

June realized something that made her chest tighten: She wasn't part of this world. Not even close.

Football wasn't just Kevin's dream—it was becoming his identity.

She felt invisible. Small. Left behind.

THE VERDICT

At the end of the trial, the lads gathered while the head coach addressed them.

"Some of you will be invited back. Some won't. That's football."

He called out a handful of names.

Kevin held his breath.

"Powers!"

Kevin nearly collapsed with relief.

THE MEDWAY YEARS

The coach continued, "You need refining. A lot. But you've got something we can work with. Be here Thursday. Same time."

Kevin nodded vigorously. "Yes, sir. Thank you, sir."

When the lads dispersed, Kevin ran to June, radiant, bouncing on his heels.

"June! Did you see? I'm in! I've got another trial session!"

She smiled, but her eyes were clouded. "That's brilliant, Kevin. Truly."

"It's happening!" he said, grabbing her hands. "This is it. This is the start. I'm going to give it everything. Everything! I'm going to train every day until—"

She gently removed her hands from his.

"Kevin," she said softly. "Don't forget about... everything else."

"What do you mean?"

"Us."

His grin faded slightly, replaced by confusion.

"June, this is football. This is my chance. I thought you'd understand."

"I do," she said. "I just... I don't want to lose you to it."

"You won't. Don't be daft."

But he was already glancing back toward the pitch, the coaches, the other lads—his new world calling to him.

THE MEDWAY YEARS

June felt it. The shift. The distance.

And as they walked out of the training ground together, Kevin talked excitedly about drills, tactics, future matches.

June walked in silence beside him, feeling like a shadow—close, present, but fading bit by bit.

She swallowed the lump in her throat. Football wasn't just taking Kevin's time. It was taking pieces of him she feared she'd never get back.

THE MEDWAY YEARS

CHAPTER SEVEN – "The Space Between Them"

The second trial session came and went. Then a third. Then informal training sessions Kevin attended even when none were required.

By early December, Kevin's world had narrowed to three things: the pitch, the ball, and the coaches' approval. Everything else—family, mates, June—fell somewhere in the foggy outside of his new, single-minded focus.

June felt it immediately.

At first it was small things.

Kevin cancelling a cinema date because he needed to "keep his legs fresh." Kevin turning up late because he stayed behind at training to perfect his passing angles. Kevin visiting her house for ten minutes, then rushing off to practice drills against the brick wall.

But soon it became larger things.

He stopped walking her home. He forgot to ask about her day.
He talked about football constantly—tactics, conditioning, trial lists, rumours about who might get signed.

And when she tried to talk about her own worries—her job, her mum's health, anything—Kevin nodded absently, eyes glazed with training schedules running in his mind.

THE MEDWAY YEARS

One evening outside her house, she said quietly, "Kevin, do you hear me at all anymore?"

"Course I do." But he couldn't repeat one thing she'd said.

June felt like a ghost—still standing there, still present, but unseen.

The obsession changed him.

He grew sharper—not physically, but emotionally. Frustration simmered just under the surface. If a coach criticised him, he brooded for hours. If a teammate outperformed him, he paced like a caged dog.

One night after a training session, he slammed the door of his house so hard the frame cracked. His father yelled, but Kevin only muttered, "He said my shooting was inconsistent. Inconsistent? I scored three out of five!"

June heard about it the next day from Barry, who commented, "Kev's wound up tighter than a drum these days."

Dougie added, "He's forgetting the rest of the world exists."

June felt her throat tighten. *She knew.*

June didn't want to confide in anyone at first—not out of pride, but because it felt like betraying Kevin. But loneliness has a way of eroding silence.

It happened one evening at the café near the station.

THE MEDWAY YEARS

Dougie was sitting alone with a mug of tea and a half-eaten sausage roll. She stepped inside to warm up and nodded to him politely. He gestured to the seat opposite him.

"Fancy some company?" he asked.

She sat. The café buzzed with quiet conversation and clinking cups.

"You look tired," Dougie said gently.

June let out a breath she hadn't meant to. "It's been a bit of a stressful week."

"Kevin?"

She nodded.

Dougie didn't push or pry. He just waited—patient, steady.

"I feel like I'm talking to myself these days," she said. "He's there, but he's not with me."

Dougie nodded slowly. "He used to be more… present."

"He used to look at me," June said softly. "Now he looks through me. Past me. Like I'm a distraction from something bigger."

"You're not a distraction," Dougie said firmly. "You're his anchor. He just can't see it right now."

She surprised herself by tearing up. She wiped her eyes quickly, embarrassed.

"Sorry."

THE MEDWAY YEARS

"You don't need to be sorry," Dougie said. "Sometimes you just need someone to hear you."

June looked at him—really looked. He had a quiet steadiness that felt like a warm blanket after weeks in the cold. Not romantic, not flirtatious—just safe.

For the first time in months, she felt noticed.

THE CONFRONTATION

Eventually, June couldn't carry her silence any longer.

She waited for Kevin outside his house after a particularly long training session. His boots were muddy, his hair damp with sweat, his face flushed from exertion. He barely noticed her as he walked up.

"Oh—June," he said, breathless. "Didn't expect you."

"Clearly."

He frowned. "What's that supposed to mean?"

"Can we talk inside?"

"Not really," Kevin said. "I've got to—"

"Kevin," she said sharply, surprising both of them. "Talk to me."

He stared at her; the first real attention he'd given her in weeks.

"What's all this about?"

THE MEDWAY YEARS

"This is about you forgetting I exist," June said, voice trembling but strong. "This is about you choosing football over everything else. Over me."

"That's not fair—"

"It is," she said. "It's the truth."

Kevin's jaw tightened. "I'm doing this for us. For our future."

"Which part of our future involves you never being around? Never listening? Never caring about anything except a ball?"

"It's my dream, June!"

"And what am I then?" she whispered. "A spare part?"

Kevin hesitated—just a moment too long.

June's heart cracked.

"I need you," she said. "Not as a footballer. As Kevin. The Kevin I knew. The one who walked me home and asked about my day and laughed at silly things."

"That Kevin's still here," he insisted.

"He's disappearing," June replied. "And I don't know how much of him will be left if this keeps going."

Kevin rubbed his face in frustration. "What do you want me to do? Quit? Give up the biggest chance of my life?"

"I want you to remember I'm in your life," she said softly. "That's all."

He didn't answer. The silence was worse than shouting. Finally, June stepped back.

THE MEDWAY YEARS

"When you're ready to be my Kevin again," she said, "you know where to find me."

She turned and walked away.

Kevin watched her go—conflicted, confused, angry at himself, angry at the world.

But he didn't run after her. He went inside.

And June, heart breaking but strangely lighter, walked toward the café, where she knew someone would listen if she needed to talk.

THE NEW CONNECTION

Later that evening, June found herself in the café again.

Dougie was there—same mug of tea, same gentle presence. He looked up as she approached.

"Rough night?" he asked.

June nodded. "You have no idea."

He slid the chair opposite him out with his foot. "Sit," he said softly. And she did.

Not because she wanted someone new— but because she needed someone who cared.

And Dougie cared.

Not romantically. Not possessively. Not expectantly. Just as Dougie.

THE MEDWAY YEARS

And right now, that was enough to keep a lonely girl from falling apart.

CHAPTER EIGHT – "Breaking the Lines"

December settled over Medway with a cold firmness, the sort that seeped into bones and made breaths come out in ghosts. But Kevin hardly noticed the weather anymore. He barely noticed anything that wasn't football.

He trained before sunrise. He trained after sunset. He trained even when his legs shook and his lungs burned.

THE MEDWAY YEARS

The coaches at Gillingham liked him—increasingly each week. But with their approval came pressure, and with pressure came something new in Kevin:

A hardness. A sharpness. A growing edge that made the others flinch.

AGGRESSION ON THE PITCH

During a scrimmage at the training ground, Kevin collided with another lad—Carter, the tall, broad player who'd mocked him on the first trial day.

It wasn't even a foul. Just shoulder to shoulder.

But Kevin snapped.

"Watch where you're going!" he barked.

Carter raised an eyebrow. "Calm down, Powers. It's football, not ballet."

Kevin shoved him. Hard.

The coach blew his whistle sharply. "Powers! Enough!"

But Kevin glared at Carter, chest heaving, fists clenched.

"You want to go?" Kevin asked quietly, dangerously.

Carter laughed, not kindly. "You're losing it, mate."

Kevin stormed off, kicking a cone so hard it flew across the pitch. The coaches exchanged looks.

Raw talent was one thing. Uncontrolled aggression was another.

THE MEDWAY YEARS

At home, Kevin's parents were walking on eggshells. He snapped at his mum for asking about his supper. He snapped at his father for suggesting he rest his ankle. He snapped at his sister for touching his football boots.

Every conversation turned into tension.

"You're not yourself," his mum said gently.

"I'm exactly who I need to be," Kevin muttered.

The more people worried, the more he shut them out. And June... June was fading from his awareness like background noise he couldn't be bothered to tune in to.

JUNE FEELS THE SHIFT

June tried. Harder than anyone would have expected of her.

She wrote him encouraging notes. She waited outside training in the cold. She offered to walk with him, cook him tea, watch him practice.

But Kevin brushed her off repeatedly.

"I don't have time tonight."

"I'm shattered, June."

"Big session tomorrow."

"Can't. Coach needs me focused."

THE MEDWAY YEARS

Her world shrank into lonely evenings and unanswered questions. She told herself he'd come back to her. He didn't.

Instead, he became someone she didn't recognise—sharp tongued, impatient, distant.

One night, after Kevin cancelled a planned dinner with her mother for the third time, June sat on her bed and felt something hollow open inside her.

I'm losing him, she thought. *Or maybe I've already lost him.*

DOUGIE'S SUPPORT

It was Dougie who noticed her slipping through the cracks. He always noticed.

One frosty evening, she passed him outside the Co-op. He had a loaf of bread tucked under one arm and a thoughtful look on his face.

"June?" he said gently. "You look… worn out."

She tried to smile. "Just tired."

"Want to talk about it?" And just like before, the dam cracked.

They walked slowly toward the river, boots crunching on grit. The lights reflected off the dark water, wavering like uncertain thoughts.

"He's changed," June said quietly. "And I don't know how to reach him."

Dougie nodded. "I've seen it. He's pushing everyone away."

THE MEDWAY YEARS

"Why?"

"Pressure," Dougie said. "Fear. Wanting something so badly it turns you inside out. But that doesn't make it fair on you."

June bit her lip. "I don't know if he even sees me anymore." Dougie stopped walking.

"He should," he said. "You're worth seeing."

June looked at him—really looked. He wasn't glamorous or ambitious. He wasn't chasing dreams bigger than the town.

But he was steady. Kind. Present.

She felt warmth bloom in her chest. A dangerous warmth. She looked away quickly.

"Thank you," she whispered.

"Any time," Dougie said. "I mean it."

THE LAST STRAW

The breaking point came on a Thursday.

June waited outside the training ground in the bitter wind, scarf pulled to her chin, breath stinging her throat. She had baked Kevin a small cake—his favourite—because she knew he'd had a tough session earlier in the week.

Kevin emerged with the other lads, laughing—properly laughing—for the first time in ages. But when he saw June, his face hardened instantly.

"What are you doing here?" he asked sharply.

THE MEDWAY YEARS

She blinked. "I... I made you something. Thought you might like—"

"I told you I had extra drills. I don't have time for this."

"For what?" June whispered. "For me?"

Kevin exhaled impatiently. "You don't get it, June. This is serious. I can't have distractions."

She stood very still. "Distractions," she repeated.

"That's not what I—"

"It's exactly what you said."

The other lads slowed, sensing tension. Kevin shifted uncomfortably.

"Look," he said, softer but unconvincing. "You know I care. But right now, I've got to think about my career."

"Your career?" June said quietly. "Kevin... you're in the *trial squad*. You're not even signed."

He flinched as if she'd slapped him.

"That's unfair."

"What's unfair," she said, voice shaking, "is that you're choosing football over everyone who cares about you. Over your family. Over your mates. Over *me*."

"I don't need this right now," Kevin snapped.

June paused. Something settled inside her, a calm she didn't expect.

THE MEDWAY YEARS

"No," she said softly. "You don't."

She placed the paper-wrapped cake at his feet.

"Good luck, Kevin. Truly. I hope you get everything you dream of."

"He opened his mouth to speak, but nothing came out." ("Introverts Struggle: Why It's Hard to Find the Right Words") June stepped back.

And turned away. And this time, Kevin didn't follow.

June Finds Herself with Dougie

Later that night, June wandered the streets in a daze. The cold bit at her cheeks, but she hardly noticed. Eventually, she found herself—without planning it—outside the café again.

Through the window, she saw Dougie. Reading the paper. Alone. Calm.

She hesitated. Then pushed the door open.

The bell above the door jingled softly. Dougie looked up, surprised at first—then concerned. "June? What's happened?"

She sat across from him, eyes shiny with unshed tears.

"It's over," she whispered.

Dougie didn't reach for her. He didn't offer clichés or false comfort. He simply said: "I'm here."

THE MEDWAY YEARS

June closed her eyes, letting the warmth of the café and Dougie's steady presence settle over her like a blanket.

For the first time in months, she felt safe. For the first time in months, she felt seen.

And somewhere deep inside, a new closeness began to grow—
quiet, tender, and impossible to ignore.

CHAPTER NINE– "Faultline"

Kevin didn't realise June was serious until the next morning.

When he woke, the usual routine played out: boots by the door, kit drying on the radiator, the ache in his calves reminding him of the night before. He expected a note from June, maybe an apology for "overreacting," something he could brush aside and then carry on as normal.

There was no note.

He checked the phone in the hall—no message. No letter pushed under the door. No soft knock on the window.

It was only then—when he reached for something that wasn't there—that the first crack appeared in him.

At first, pride stepped in. "She'll come around," he muttered.

He told himself June was emotional. Sensitive. He had *real* things to focus on. But when he arrived at the training ground, expecting to see her by the fence as usual, the empty space hit him like a cold hand gripping his throat.

THE MEDWAY YEARS

Carter smirked from across the pitch. "Where's the missus today, Powers? Finally fed up with you?"

Kevin's jaw tightened. "Shut it."

But Carter wasn't wrong. June wasn't there.

Throughout training, Kevin's passes were heavy. His shots went wide. His concentration fractured like thin ice.

"Head in the game, Powers!" the coach barked. "You're not on your own pitch now!"

Kevin nodded, but the words cut through him. He wasn't in his game. He wasn't in anything.

After training, he checked the streets on the walk home. Her usual route. Her window. The café. Nothing.

By early afternoon, heartbreak overtook pride—all at once, like a dam bursting. He sat on the river wall, elbows on knees, staring at the rippling grey water.

She's really gone. Not dead, not lost—just absent. And absence was its own kind of pain.

A QUIET FLAME

June hadn't meant to see Dougie again so soon. But life often places people where they need to be, not where they expect.

Two days after leaving Kevin, June and Brenda wandered through town, arms full of shopping bags, trying to distract

THE MEDWAY YEARS

June from her misery. When they approached The Riverview café, Brenda spotted Dougie through the window.

"There's your shadow," Brenda teased. June blushed. "He's just… kind."

"Kindness is rare," Brenda replied, "and valuable."

Inside, Dougie looked up from his tea and smiled—a small, genuine smile that warmed June more than she wanted to admit.

Brenda nudged her. "Go on." June approached timidly. "Mind if we join?"

"'Course not," Dougie said, already pulling out chairs.

Brenda slipped away quickly—far too quickly. "Actually, I've got to pick something up. You two catch up!"

June shot her a glare; Brenda winked and disappeared.

Dougie watched June sit, noticing the tiredness in her eyes. "You holding up?" he asked gently.

June nodded, though her lip trembled. "Trying."

"You don't have to pretend with me."

She exhaled shakily, eyes watering before she could stop them. Dougie pushed his mug toward her without a word.

"Warm your hands. My treat."

She held the mug, letting the heat seep into her palms like reassurance. "I didn't think it would hurt this much," she whispered.

THE MEDWAY YEARS

"It hurts most when you fight for someone who stops fighting for you," Dougie said quietly.

June's eyes flicked to his. "You always say the right thing."

"I say what I see."

"What do you see now?"

Dougie hesitated, then said softly: "I see someone who deserves better than being second place to a dream."

June looked at him—really looked—and something fragile, tender, and dangerous shimmered between them.

Not romance. Not yet. But the spark of something real.

TENSIONS RISE

Word spread quickly through the group. Kevin and June had split. June wasn't crying or hiding—she was out in town with Dougie. Talking to him. Laughing sometimes. Looking steadier.

Barry was the first to comment, pulling Dougie aside near the shops.

"Mate… be careful."

"Careful of what?" Dougie asked.

"You know what I mean. People are watching."

Dougie frowned. "I'm not doing anything wrong."

THE MEDWAY YEARS

"I know," Barry said. "But Kevin? He's wound tight as piano wire. Finding out June's spending time with you—he won't take it well."

Dougie's stomach tightened. "It's not like that."

"It won't matter what it's *like*. Only what it looks like."

Later that evening, Brenda whispered conspiratorially in June's ear:

"You and Dougie make a good pair."

June flushed. "Stop. It isn't like that."

Brenda raised an eyebrow. "If you say so."

Even Martin got involved, tossing a grape at Dougie at the dance hall. "So, what's this I hear about you and June sharing romantic cups of tea?" he teased.

Dougie groaned. "Martin, for once in your life, shut up." Martin blinked, actually surprised by Dougie's sharpness.

KEVIN HEARS THE RUMOUR

It didn't take long for the gossip to reach Kevin. He overheard two lads at training.

"Powers' girl's been seen with that Barnes bloke."

"Barnes? The quiet one?"

"Yeah. They've been close lately."

"Think she's moved on already?"

THE MEDWAY YEARS

Laughter.

Something cold and furious snapped inside Kevin.

He grabbed Carter by the shirt during a challenge later, slamming him into the turf.

The coach blew his whistle furiously. "Powers! Off the pitch! NOW!"

But Kevin barely heard him. His pulse roared in his ears. His heart was hammering like fists against a locked door.

June…………..and Dougie. He stormed from the training ground before the coach could finish shouting.

That evening, Kevin stood outside Dougie's house, fists clenched, breath fogging in the chilly air.

He didn't knock. Not yet. He just stood there—wounded pride, heartbreak, suspicion, and fear all tangled inside his chest.

Inside, Dougie sat with June and Brenda, the three of them laughing softly at a joke Martin had made earlier. But outside, Kevin whispered to the darkness:

"Barnes… what are you doing?"

His voice cracked. "And why with her?"

A SHIFT IN THE AIR

THE MEDWAY YEARS

As Dougie walked June home later that evening—talking easily, naturally—neither noticed the figure watching them from the shadows near the old lamppost.

Kevin. Eyes red. Jaw clenched so tight he thought it might break.

He watched Dougie gently place a hand on June's arm to steady her over a puddle. He watched June lean in to listen to something Dougie murmured. He watched their silhouettes move closer than two friends normally would.

Something inside him shattered. Not anger. Not jealousy. A hollow, devastating ache of realisation:

He'd pushed her away. And she'd found comfort in someone else's presence.

Someone better at listening. Better at caring. Better at being human.

Kevin turned and walked into the night—lost, furious, and ashamed—leaving the two of them under the streetlamp, unaware of the storm gathering outside their small, fragile bond.

THE MEDWAY YEARS

CHAPTER TEN – "Lines Drawn in Quiet Places"

The group had always been tight woven together through years of school corridors, dance halls, riverbanks, and street corners. But in the weeks after Kevin and June's breakup, something subtle and dangerous began to seep into the spaces between them.

Not arguments. Not shouting. Just... *differences.* Quiet ones.
But strong enough to pull friendships in opposite directions.

The old café by the station had always been their meeting spot—one long table, too small for how many of them squeezed around it, cups of tea cooling beside plates of toast.

But now, the seating had changed.

On one side sat Dougie, June, Brenda, and Jackie.

On the other side, Barry and Brian—keeping a sort of neutral ground—while Martin floated between them depending on who bought him breakfast.

Kevin, of course, hadn't been in the café for weeks. He barely spoke to anyone now.

That morning, the group trickled in slowly. June arrived with Brenda. Dougie was already there. Jackie joined shortly after.

THE MEDWAY YEARS

Barry looked between the clusters of seats, uncertain.

"So," he said awkwardly, "are we splitting the table in half now like some schoolroom rivalry?"

Jackie rolled her eyes. "Oh, stop it. No one's doing sides."

Brenda coughed softly. "Aren't we, though?"

Barry frowned. "It's not sides. It's… awkwardness."

Brian nodded. "Yeah. Kev's wound up like a spring. And Dougie—well…"

He didn't finish the sentence, because Martin plopped into the nearest seat and declared, "I'm sitting in Switzerland. Fully neutral. I will accept bribes."

No one laughed. Even Martin felt the shift and slowly lowered his teacup.

LITTLE COMMENTS WITH WEIGHT

It started with whispering—not malicious, but tense. Jackie leaned close to Brenda. "He'll come after Dougie, you know."

"Kevin?" Brenda whispered. "He's all bark."

Jackie shook her head. "No. He's different now. Angrier."

Across the table, Brian muttered to Barry, "Dougie shouldn't be getting this close. Even if nothing's happening, it looks bad."

Barry sighed. "He's not doing anything wrong."

THE MEDWAY YEARS

"That won't matter to Kevin."

Barry rubbed his forehead. "Christ. We sound like gossips." But the truth hung between them:

They were talking about Kevin in the way people talk about a storm gathering over the river—inevitable yet unpredictable.

Dougie wasn't oblivious. He noticed how Brian's eyes lingered on him a second too long. How Barry hesitated before speaking. How Martin made fewer jokes when June sat beside Dougie. How Jackie and Brenda whispered with concern whenever June reached for his arm.

He wasn't doing anything improper. But sometimes innocence doesn't look like innocence.

One afternoon, while Dougie waited for June outside her workplace, Barry approached him, hands in pockets.

"Mate," Barry said quietly, "you need to be careful."

Dougie sighed. "I know what you're going to say."

"Then you know I'm not saying it because I'm judging. I'm saying it because I'm your mate."

Dougie stared at the ground. "I don't want trouble."

"I know," Barry said softly. "But trouble's looking for you."

June could feel the divide too.

THE MEDWAY YEARS

When she entered the Riverview dance hall one Saturday night with Brenda, she felt the air change around her.

Brian gave her a polite nod. Jackie hugged her quickly. Martin waved, relieved to see her. But when she sat by Dougie, conversations quietened. It wasn't hostile. Just uncertain.

June leaned close to Dougie. "They're uncomfortable."

Dougie kept his eyes on the dance floor. "They think it's… something."

"Is it?" she whispered.

Dougie paused. "No. But I care about you. And that's enough for people to talk."

June swallowed hard. "I hate this."

"It's not your fault."

"It's not yours either."

But blame didn't matter. Perception did.

KEVIN RETURNS

The real crack formed the night Kevin finally showed up again—unexpected, unannounced, and completely changed.

He entered the Riverview alone, shoulders hunched, eyes sunken from lack of sleep. He didn't go to the bar. He didn't

THE MEDWAY YEARS

greet anyone. He just stood at the edge of the dance floor, scanning the room. Looking.

He spotted June beside Dougie.

Everything stopped for him. Breath. Thought. Sense.

June froze when she noticed him. Dougie slowly stood up.

Barry moved closer instinctively, ready to step in.

Brian watched with sharp attention.

Martin swallowed hard and muttered, "Here we go…"

Kevin didn't speak. He didn't shout. He didn't make a scene.

He just stared—with hurt, with disbelief, with a storm packed tight behind his eyes. Then he turned around and walked out.

June's chest tightened painfully. Dougie's stomach dropped. The group exchanged anxious glances.

No one followed Kevin. No one dared.

But the air in the hall felt shattered.

Aftermath

When Kevin left, the group broke into whispers.

Jackie murmured, "He looked awful."

Brian shook his head. "He looked angry."

Brenda said, "He looked… lost."

Barry stared at Dougie. "You have to speak to him."

77

THE MEDWAY YEARS

Dougie shook his head. "He won't listen to me."

"You don't have a choice," Barry replied. "This is going to blow up."

June's voice cracked as she whispered, "Please... don't fight."

Dougie took her hand gently—not romantic, just steady.

"I won't fight him," he said. "But he might want to fight me."

Martin cleared his throat. "We should just all... you know... breathe a bit. Give it time."

But time wasn't healing anything. It was only making the lines clearer.

Barry, Brian, and Martin felt loyalty tugging them toward Kevin—even if they didn't like his behaviour.

Brenda, Jackie, and—more quietly—Maureen leaned toward June, trying to shield her from Kevin's anger and heartbreak.

And Dougie? Dougie stood right in the middle. Caught between friendship and compassion. Between loyalty and honesty. Between two hearts breaking in separate ways.

The group had always been one circle. Now it was two. And each week, those halves drifted farther apart— pulled apart by silence, suspicion, and a love story that had quietly changed shape.

THE MEDWAY YEARS

CHAPTER ELEVEN – "Collision"

The confrontation didn't happen in a dance hall or at the café, or even at the training ground where tempers ran hot.

It happened late—late—on a freezing Wednesday night in January, when the streets were quiet and the river mist curled low and grey over the pavements.

Dougie had stayed late with Barry, helping him shift some crates behind his uncle's shop. By the time they finished, the cold had seeped into Dougie's bones. He pulled his collar up and started the long walk home.

He didn't realise someone was following him. Not until a voice—sharp, cutting—broke the silence behind him.

"Barnes."

Dougie froze. Turned. And saw Kevin.

Kevin looked… wrong. Thin. Pale. Eyes dark with lack of sleep and something far worse—jealousy, confusion, grief.

His coat hung loose on him. His hair was unkempt. And his entire posture looked like a man held together with fraying rope. Dougie swallowed. "Kevin."

Kevin stepped closer, hands shaking slightly—not from cold, but from whatever emotion was eating him alive.

"You and me," Kevin said quietly. "We need a talk."

Dougie nodded cautiously. "All right."

THE MEDWAY YEARS

But Kevin wasn't calm. Not even close.

Kevin clenched and unclenched his fists. "I saw you. With her."

Dougie's stomach tightened. "Kevin, please listen—"

"You think I'm stupid?"

"No. I don't."

"Then why are you sneaking around with June?" Kevin demanded, stepping closer. "Why are you—what—comforting her? Walking her home? Taking my place?"

"I'm not taking your place," Dougie said firmly.

"You are!" Kevin snapped. "You are, and everyone sees it but you!"

Dougie felt the night tighten around them, air sharp with tension.

"She needed someone, Kev. You pushed her away."

Kevin's face twisted. "Don't. Don't you dare talk like you understand anything about her and me."

"I understand she was hurting," Dougie said softly. "And alone."

Kevin's jaw clenched hard. "And you were right there."

Dougie hesitated. "I was just being her friend."

Kevin laughed—harsh, brittle. "You? Her friend?"

THE MEDWAY YEARS

He stepped so close Dougie could feel the heat of his breath in the cold.

"You want her," Kevin said quietly. "Don't you?"

Dougie didn't answer immediately. And that silence—tiny, hesitant—was exactly the wrong answer.

Kevin's eyes went wild.

Kevin shoved him. Hard. Dougie stumbled backward, boots scraping on the frosty pavement.

"Kev—!"
"No!" Kevin roared. "Don't say my name like you care!"

He shoved him again—harder, angrier, years of insecurity pouring out.

"You think you're better than me?"
"No."
"You think you can step in and fix everything?"
"No, I—"
"You think she needs you? *You?*"

Dougie raised his hands in surrender. "Kevin, please—"

Kevin swung a wild, uncontrolled punch, which grazed Dougie's cheek and sent him staggering to the wall beside the river steps.

"Kev!" Dougie shouted. "Stop!"

But Kevin's pain had turned into fury—raw, unfiltered, and blinding.

THE MEDWAY YEARS

"You betrayed me," Kevin said, voice breaking. "You were my mate. You were supposed to be on my side."

"I *am* on your side!"

Kevin punched him again—this time full contact. Dougie felt his lip split, the metallic tang of blood filling his mouth.

"Stop it!" Dougie shouted, grabbing Kevin's wrists. "Kevin, stop!"

They grappled—Dougie never striking back, just trying to hold Kevin still.

Kevin's breath came in ragged, guttural gasps. "Why her, Dougie? Why did it have to be her?"

"Because she needed someone, Kev," Dougie said desperately. "And you weren't there."

Something broke in Kevin at those words. Not anger. Not pride. Grief.

He sagged, fists loosening, body trembling, breath shuddering in and out.

Dougie released him slowly, cautiously.

Kevin staggered backward, eyes shining with tears that he tried and failed to blink away.

"I loved her," Kevin whispered.

"I know," Dougie said softly, wiping the blood from his lip. "I know you did."

"I still do."

THE MEDWAY YEARS

"I know."

Kevin stared at him—a long, silent, tortured stare. Then he shook his head.

"You shouldn't have taken her side," Kevin said, voice small and broken.

And before Dougie could answer, Kevin turned and walked into the darkness—shoulders hunched, footsteps uneven, pain trailing behind him like a long shadow.

AFTERMATH

Dougie stood there in the cold, lip throbbing, heart heavy.

He didn't feel victorious. Or angry. Or self-righteous.

He felt… sorrow. For Kevin. For June. For himself. For the group that was fracturing one piece at a time.

Barry found him twenty minutes later, jogging breathlessly across the bridge after hearing raised voices from the docks.

"Dougie! What the hell happened? Are you—?"

Dougie simply shook his head. "Kev," he whispered.

Barry's face went pale. "Did he hurt you?"

Dougie touched his swollen lip. "A bit. But he's hurting more."

Barry swore softly under his breath. "This is bad, Dougie. Really bad."

"I know."

THE MEDWAY YEARS

The river flowed quietly beside them, indifferent to the turmoil of boys becoming men too soon.

By the next day, the whole group knew.

Brenda cried when she saw Dougie's bruised lip. Jackie fretted. Brian muttered something about Kevin "losing himself." Martin fell silent for once, unusually pale.

June, when she heard, covered her mouth with her hand, tears pooling in her eyes. "He hit you?" she whispered.

"He was hurting," Dougie said gently. "It wasn't really about me."

June's voice cracked. "I'm so sorry."

"You didn't do anything wrong."

But Kevin had. And now the group wasn't just divided. It was broken.

CHAPTER TWELVE – "Bruises and Boundaries"

Dougie woke the next morning to a dull, throbbing ache along his jaw and a stiff tightness in his lip. The cold mug of tea on his bedside table told him he'd fallen asleep without meaning to. His mother had already gone to work, leaving a note downstairs:

THE MEDWAY YEARS

Saw your lip. If you get into fights, don't expect sympathy. Food is in the oven. Be sensible. – Mum

Dougie sighed. He hadn't been *in* a fight. He'd just stood in the middle of one.

There was a knock on the door around mid-morning.

Soft. Uneven. Hesitant. Dougie opened it and froze.

"June," he whispered.

She stood on the doorstep wrapped in a blue coat, hair tied back, cheeks flushed from the cold. Her eyes widened when she saw his face.

"Oh, Dougie…"

He tried to smile. "Looks worse than it is."

"It looks awful," she said quietly.

She stepped inside without waiting to be invited—an instinctive, caring movement. Dougie felt his heart shift painfully at the sight.

"Sit," she said, gently guiding him to the table.

He obeyed without argument.

She opened her bag and took out cotton wool, a small bottle of antiseptic, and a clean handkerchief. "Brenda told me what happened," June murmured, dabbing the cotton gently along his split lip. "I'm so sorry."

"Don't be," Dougie said. "You didn't hit me."

THE MEDWAY YEARS

"That doesn't mean I'm not part of the reason," she whispered.

Dougie reached up, catching her wrist lightly. "You're not a reason for anything bad, June."

She froze at the touch, eyes meeting his. It lingered—just for a heartbeat—before she pulled her hand back softly and continued cleaning the wound.

She worked with careful precision, her breath warm as she leaned close. Dougie could smell her shampoo—lavender and something sweet. June muttered, "He had no right. Kevin had no right to do this to you."

"He wasn't himself."

"That's no excuse."

Dougie exhaled slowly. "He's hurting."

"So are you."

Dougie paused. "That's different."

June looked at him, really looked at him, and something melted in her expression. "You always put yourself last," she said softly.

"I don't think about it."

"That's exactly my point."

She finished tending to the wounds, then sat beside him, hands resting in her lap. "I care about you, Dougie," she said quietly.

THE MEDWAY YEARS

He felt his breath catch. "June… I care about you too. A lot."

The air grew warm, heavy—not romantic, but intimate. Two people leaning toward each other without realising it, without meaning to, but unable to help it.

June broke the moment first, looking away. "I don't know what happens next."

"Neither do I," Dougie admitted. "But I'm not going to push you. Or rush you."

June nodded appreciatively. "Thank you. For being gentle with me."

THE GROUP'S ATTEMPT AT PEACE

Later that afternoon, Barry gathered whoever he could find. Martin. Jackie. Brenda. Brian eventually wandered over, hands in pockets.

They met at the small green near the church—neutral ground.

Barry rubbed the back of his neck. "We need to sort this mess."

Martin blew out a breath. "By 'sort' you mean 'prevent Kevin from knocking someone else's teeth out,' right?"

"Especially Dougie's," Brenda added, glancing anxiously at Dougie's swollen lip.

Brian nodded. "Kev's going to lose it again. He's barely holding anything together."

THE MEDWAY YEARS

Jackie reached for Barry's arm. "Maybe June should talk to him. She could calm him down."

June, sitting quietly beside Dougie, tensed at the suggestion.

"No," she said firmly. "I'm not going back to being shouted at. I'm not the solution to Kevin's temper."

Brian sighed. "Fair enough. But someone has to talk to him."

All eyes turned to Barry. He held up his hands immediately. "Oh no. I'm not his keeper."

"But you're the closest thing he has," Jackie said gently.

Barry groaned. "I'll try. But I'm telling you, he's not going to take it well."

"Better than taking it out on Dougie," Martin muttered.

Dougie shook his head. "Don't go on about me. This is about Kevin."

"No," June said, touching Dougie's arm, "it's about all of us. We're coming apart."

There was a heavy silence. She was right. They all felt it.

The group—once inseparable—now sat in two clumps, separated by unspoken tension.

Barry stood. "Fine. I'll give it a go. But don't keep your hopes up."

THE MEDWAY YEARS

Barry found Kevin behind the training ground that evening, kicking a ball repeatedly against a brick wall—harder each time, like trying to break something that wouldn't break.

"Kevin," Barry called out cautiously. The ball rebounded. Kevin caught it without looking.

"What do you want?"

"We need to talk."

"Not interested."

"It's about Dougie."

Kevin's shoulders tensed like steel cables.

Barry held up his hands. "Kev, listen. He wasn't—"

"He was with her," Kevin snapped. "Don't tell me what he was or wasn't doing."

"He didn't do anything wrong."

Kevin turned, eyes blazing. "I'll decide what's wrong."

"Kev… please. Calm down. You'll ruin everything. Gillingham, your life, your—"

Kevin grabbed Barry by the jacket, slamming him against the wall.

"Don't tell me about my life," Kevin hissed. "You don't know anything about it."

Barry didn't fight back—he simply stared at his old friend with stunned heartbreak.

THE MEDWAY YEARS

Kevin released him a moment later, chest heaving.

Barry straightened his coat. "This isn't you."

Kevin frowned. "Maybe this *is* me."

"No," Barry said quietly. "It's who you're becoming. And it's going to destroy you."

Kevin kicked the ball hard—so hard it sailed into the trees and disappeared.

"Get out of here," he muttered. "All of you. Leave me alone."

Barry walked away slowly, the weight of failure pulling at his steps.

When Barry returned to the green, the group looked up anxiously.

"Well?" Martin asked.

Barry shook his head. "It's no good. He's beyond listening."

June closed her eyes slowly, pain washing over her.

Dougie reached for her hand. She didn't pull away.

Brenda took Jackie's hand for comfort. Brian stared at the ground, jaw tight. Even Martin looked unusually subdued.

Barry sank onto the grass. "He's angry at all of us. But mostly at himself."

"And Dougie," Brian added.

Dougie swallowed hard. "I don't want him as an enemy."

THE MEDWAY YEARS

June squeezed his fingers gently. "You're not the enemy. He's fighting himself more than anyone."

The group exchanged glances—united in fear, uncertainty, and sadness. But not united in spirit.

They were together, physically. But emotionally, they stood on opposite sides of an invisible faultline. One that had already begun to crack.

CHAPTER THIRTEEN – "The Night the Music Died"

The Medway Winter Dance was the biggest social event of the season. Held in the decorated hall behind the church, it was a night when the whole town came together—new dresses, polished shoes, tables of sandwiches and jelly, the works.

The band—*The Riverbeats*—was playing, filling the hall with lively echoes of 1961 rock and roll. People laughed, danced, spun under the lights. For a moment, the world outside felt far away.

But for the group, the atmosphere was tight with unsaid things.

June and Brenda arrived together, wearing their best dresses.

Dougie followed with Martin and Barry, trying to function as

THE MEDWAY YEARS

if nothing had changed. Brian and Jackie drifted in moments later. But one seat at their usual table stayed empty. Kevin's.

Until it didn't.

KEVIN'S ARRIVAL

He entered halfway through the second set.

Heads turned. People whispered.

He looked sharp—hair slicked, suit neat—but his eyes betrayed him. They were wild, tired, feverish with emotion he hadn't been able to swallow. He scanned the hall with a predator's patience. Found June. Found Dougie. And began walking toward them.

June stiffened. Dougie's stomach dropped. Barry murmured, "Christ, here we go…"

Kevin stopped at their table.

His gaze burned into June. Then shifted to Dougie. His voice was low, but deadly calm. "Get up."

Dougie stayed seated. "Kevin… let's talk outside."

"No," Kevin said. "We talk here."

The hall fell quieter as everyone sensed the tension.

Martin coughed nervously. "Kev, mate—let's not do this—"

"Shut up, Martin," Kevin snapped.

Martin shrank back.

THE MEDWAY YEARS

Kevin leaned closer to Dougie. "You think you can take everything from me? First June. Then my mates. Now what? My dignity too?"

Dougie shook his head slowly. "No one took anything from you. You pushed it away."

Kevin's face twisted. "Shut up."

June stood quickly. "Kevin—please. Stop this."

His eyes flared. "You don't get to talk."

The entire table froze. Even the band stopped playing.

June's voice trembled. "I'm not yours anymore. You don't own me. You can't order me to be silent."

Kevin slammed a hand on the table. Glass rattled. People gasped.

"YOU LEFT ME!" he shouted.

"And you gave me no choice!" June cried.

The hall fell into a suffocating silence.

Kevin turned back to Dougie.

"So, what now? Do you think you're her knight in shining armour? You think you can step into my life and pretend you're doing me a favour?"

Dougie rose slowly, trying to stay calm. "I never tried to be anything but your friend."

"Liar," Kevin spat.

THE MEDWAY YEARS

Then— without warning— Kevin swung. But this time, Dougie didn't manage to dodge.

The punch hit him full in the cheek. June screamed. The crowd   gasped.
Barry and Brian lunged forward to restrain Kevin, but he shoved them off with surprising strength.

Dougie stumbled backward into a table, glass crashing to the floor. Brenda covered her mouth in horror. Jackie cried out. Martin froze, pale as chalk.

Kevin went for Dougie again—fists raised, breath ragged— but Barry grabbed him around the waist. Brian seized his arms.

"Kev! STOP!" Barry shouted. "You're going to hurt someone!" Brian yelled.

Kevin thrashed wildly, tears and fury mixing unchecked.

"Let me go!" he roared. "He took everything from me! EVERYTHING!"

June fell to her knees beside Dougie as he pressed a hand to his jaw, blood on his lip again.

"Are you all right?" she whispered, voice cracking.

"I'll be fine," Dougie managed.

Kevin saw her kneeling there, touching Dougie's face, and his rage reached breaking point.

"YOU!" he screamed. "You chose HIM?"

THE MEDWAY YEARS

June stood, eyes fierce for the first time. "I chose peace, Kevin. You gave me pain."

Her words hit harder than any punch. Kevin went still. Then something shattered inside him.

THE FINAL BLOW

Two Gillingham scouts—who happened to be attending the dance with their wives—had witnessed the entire incident. They exchanged grim looks and whispered urgently to each other.

Brian, still holding Kevin back, noticed them and swore under his breath. "Kev," he said urgently into Kevin's ear, "you've just made a huge mistake."

"What?" Kevin panted.

"Those two men," Brian whispered. "They're from Gillingham."

Kevin's breath froze. He turned his head slowly.

The scouts were watching him. Disappointment clear as daylight. One shook his head slightly.

Then they looked away without a word.

Kevin's knees buckled.

If Barry and Brian weren't holding him, he might've collapsed.

THE MEDWAY YEARS

THE TURNING POINT

Kevin's voice broke. "No… no, no, no…"

Barry lowered him slowly to sit on the floor. His rage had dissolved— replaced by horror.

"What have I done?" Kevin whispered. His hands shook violently. "What did I DO?"

Barry swallowed hard. "You let your anger ruin the one thing you cared about."

Kevin stared to see where the scouts were, but they had left. His future was slipping away. Not because of Dougie. Not because of June.

Because of himself.

The hall began to buzz again—whispers, stares, judgement.

People avoided Kevin. Others murmured under their breath. The band nervously resumed playing, though the joy was gone.

Brian sighed deeply. "We need to get him out of here."

Barry nodded. "Come on, Kev."

They lifted him gently.

Kevin didn't resist. He didn't speak. He looked empty—like someone who'd lost more than a fight.

As they took him away, June turned to Dougie.

THE MEDWAY YEARS

"I'm so sorry," she whispered.

"It's not your fault," Dougie said.

But his cheek ached. His heart ached more.

When the boys disappeared out the door with Kevin, Martin exhaled shakily.

"Well," he said quietly. "That's it, then. The group… it'll never be the same." And for once — Martin was absolutely right.

PART TWO

CHAPTER FOURTEEN – "The Summer of '66"

The Medway towns looked different in 1966. Not entirely changed—still the chimneys, the chatter, the river sliding past like a lazy memory—but polished somehow, brightened by the energy of a new era. England was buzzing with World Cup fever, transistor radios crackling in every open window, children kicking battered footballs down narrow streets pretending to be Bobby Charlton or Geoff Hurst.

And among the crowds and commotion, the old gang— scattered now—each carried their own stories.

KEVIN – FINDING HIS FEET AGAIN

Kevin Powers walked through Chatham High Street with a steadier stride than he'd had in years. The darkness that once haunted him had eased; the sharpness in his eyes softened. He'd rebuilt himself slowly after the collapse in

THE MEDWAY YEARS

'62—first with sporadic labour jobs, then with coaching little kids down the park on weekends, where he realised he still loved football—but without the poison of obsession.

Now, in July 1966, he held something almost sacred: **two tickets to the World Cup Final at Wembley Stadium.**

He kept checking his jacket pocket, half expecting them to vanish.

People looked at him differently these days—like he was simply Kevin again. Not the angry boy who threw punches at dances. Not the failed trialist. Just Kevin Powers, bit rough around the edges, but decent again. He'd regained something he thought he'd lost forever: **his dignity.**

And he'd decided: He would offer one ticket to Dougie.

It wasn't just generosity. It was healing.

DOUGIE & JUNE – A HOME OF THEIR OWN

In a small, terraced house in Gillingham, **June Barnes** carried little **Karen** in her arms, swaying gently as she hummed. Karen was just past her first birthday—bright-eyed, curly-haired, and already grabbing everything within reach.

Dougie came in from work, smelling faintly of machine oil and fresh air. He kissed Karen first, then June, the ease of routine settling into his shoulders.

"Someone missed you," June said with a grin.

Karen gurgled, reaching for Dougie's face.

THE MEDWAY YEARS

He took her, bouncing her lightly. "And how's my little troublemaker?"

Their home was simple but full of warmth—flowers on the table, washing drying near the stove, June's sewing machine in the corner. Dougie had matured into a quiet family man, steady and content. June loved him for that steadiness. After the chaos with Kevin a few years years ago, this peace felt earned.

But sometimes—usually on Sunday evenings—Dougie looked out the window a bit longer than usual. Not regret. Just memory.

June knew. She'd lived those memories too. But they'd chosen peace together. And it had become their world.

TONY – THE ROAD BACK

Further down Rochester Road, Tony Marks stood outside a meeting hall, adjusting the collar of his shirt. A blue-and-white sign above the door read: **Alcoholics Anonymous – Tuesday & Friday Meetings**

He took a long breath before stepping inside.

He wasn't ashamed—not anymore. Shame had been part of the old Tony: the boy Maggie left behind, the man who drowned heartbreak in bottle after bottle until he lost jobs, friends, and himself.

But recovery had taught him something profound: What happens to you isn't your fault. What you do next is.

THE MEDWAY YEARS

Still tall, still sharp-featured, but gentler now, Tony attended every meeting he could. He spoke little, listened often. The shakes were gone. The anger too. And though he still lived alone, he was no longer lonely.

He'd sometimes pass old familiar places—the café, The Riverview—and feel a tug in his chest. Not for Maggie, not anymore. But for who he had been before everything fell apart. Youth isn't a place to which you can return.

Tony lived just one day at a time. And most days were good.

That was enough for now.

BRENDA

No one saw much of Brenda Watson anymore. In '63 she'd shocked them all by joining the **Women's Royal Naval Service**, leaving Medway behind for Portsmouth, then Plymouth, then Edinburgh. Her letters were infrequent but warm—telling stories of life on the base, of officers who treated her well, of friends she'd made from all corners of Britain.

She wrote to Dougie once, in 1965: *I'm proud of you, you know. You turned out steadier than any of us expected. Give my love to June.*

And that was the last letter. Sometimes Jackie wondered if Brenda would ever return home. But some people, she said to herself, are meant to keep moving.

THE MEDWAY YEARS

MARTIN – A FALL AND A FADING

Then there was Martin Prentice.

Once the joker of the group, the boy who lit up rooms with mischief and laughter—now he was quieter, older than his years. His six-month prison sentence in '64 had changed him in ways most didn't understand.

He'd come out thin, subdued, embarrassed. He avoided the old streets where people whispered. He kept his head down. The humour was still there, somewhere beneath the surface, but dimmer—like a once-bright lamp now flickering.

Barry still checked on him every fortnight. "You all right, Mart?"
Martin always answered, "Yeah, mate. Still here."

But there was distance in his eyes. A loneliness nobody knew how to reach.

By July 1966, their lives had diverged so far the group was barely a group at all. Just threads of memory stretching between different futures. But all of Britain was buzzing for the World Cup Final, and in Medway, the old friendships stirred faintly under the excitement, like embers that refused to die out completely.

Kevin held the tickets. England were in the final. Something in the air—optimism, nostalgia, fate—was pulling the past forward. And soon, the old gang would find themselves reconnecting, drawn together by the energy of that summer—and by choices yet to be made.

THE MEDWAY YEARS

CHAPTER FIFTEEN – "Kevin's Gesture"

Kevin walked the length of Gillingham High Street, tickets safely tucked into his inside pocket, rehearsing the words he hadn't said in years.

Dougie… I'm sorry. Dougie, I was wrong. Dougie, I'd like you to come with me to Wembley.

None of them sounded right. But he kept walking.

He reached Dougie and June's house around teatime. Smoke curled from the chimney. Light spilled gently from the windows. He heard soft baby laughter from inside.

He hesitated. Turned as if to leave. Stopped himself. He knocked.

June opened the door holding Karen, who reached out to him immediately—babies never judged anyone.

"Kevin," June said softly, surprised but not unkind. "It's been a while."

"It has." Kevin smiled awkwardly. "Is Dougie in?"

June studied him for a moment. Saw the humility, the nerves, the sincerity. Then she stepped aside.

"He's in the living room. Go on."

Kevin entered, hat in hand, heart thudding.

Dougie stood when he saw him. Not defensive. Not wary. Just older. Steadier.

THE MEDWAY YEARS

"Kev," Dougie said. "It's good to see you."

Kevin swallowed. He hadn't expected kindness. He didn't feel he deserved it.

"I've got something to ask you," Kevin said. "Something big."

Dougie gestured to the sofa. "Sit, mate."

Kevin sat. Hands shaking, he pulled the two tickets from his pocket and placed them on the table.

Dougie's eyes widened. "Is that—?"

"Wembley," Kevin said quietly. "The final."

Dougie picked one up as if it were fragile. "Kev... these must've cost—"

"They did," Kevin said, smiling faintly. "Saved months for them."

"Who's the other for?" Dougie asked gently.

Kevin met his eyes. Yours. But he didn't say it yet. Had to get the words right.

"It's time I sorted things out," Kevin said. "Made peace. With you. With whom I was."

Dougie nodded slowly. "I'd like that."

Kevin exhaled shakily. He felt lighter already.

"The other ticket is yours," he said.

Dougie blinked. "Mine?"

Kevin nodded. "If you'll have it. And if you'll have… me. As a friend again."

Silence. Then Dougie smiled—the same warm, steady smile he'd had since they were boys. "Course I will," he said. "Always did."

June watched from the doorway, eyes misty with relief.

And little Karen clapped her hands as if cheering for the return of something precious.

CHAPTER SIXTEEN – "Wembley '66"

The morning of the World Cup Final dawned bright and warm, with a sky as blue as a Chelsea football club shirt. In

THE MEDWAY YEARS

Medway, radios crackled with excitement, streets hummed with chatter, and families hung red-and-white bunting from their windows.

Dougie stood outside his house with a packed lunch June insisted on making.

"Just in case you don't want to pay London prices," she'd said, handing him sandwiches wrapped in greaseproof paper.

June kissed him on the cheek. "Have the best time."

Kevin arrived moments later, looking sharp in a clean white shirt and blazer—more put-together than Dougie had seen him in years. "You ready?" Kevin asked.

Dougie nodded. "More than ready."

Kevin offered a shy smile. "Let's go, mate."

And for the first time since they were boys, they walked side by side with ease.

THE TRAIN NORTH

The train from Chatham to London Bridge station was already overflowing with fans—men waving flags, women with painted cheeks, kids bouncing with anticipation. People sang *"Three Lions"* before it even existed, humming makeshift chants and laughing loudly.

THE MEDWAY YEARS

Kevin and Dougie squeezed into a seat, sharing the cramped space with two elderly gentlemen who carried a battered thermos and a radio held together with tape.

"You lads off to Wembley then?" one asked.

"That obvious?" Dougie smiled.

"Everyone's off to Wembley today," the old man grinned.

The train clattered along the tracks, rattling through Higham, Strood, Gravesend, Dartford, Charlton,—each station swelling the crowd, each stop adding to the roar of voices.

Kevin looked out of the window, sun hitting his eyes.

"Feels strange," he said quietly. "Coming back here with you. After everything."

Dougie nodded. "Feels right though."

Kevin's throat tightened. "Thanks for giving me another chance."

"You gave yourself one," Dougie replied.

Kevin didn't respond. He just smiled—a real, grateful smile.

WEMBLEY RISING

THE MEDWAY YEARS

When they stepped off the train at London Bridge station, the air crackled with excitement. They got the tube over to Wembley Central.

Crowds flowed toward the stadium in a river of red-and-white scarves. Vendors sold rosettes, rattles, and tiny paper flags. The smell of frying onions and beer hung in the warm air.

Then the stadium appeared, massive, white towers gleaming, crowds circling it like worshippers around a cathedral. Kevin stopped walking.

"Look at it," he whispered. "I've dreamed of this place since I was a kid."

Dougie placed a hand on his shoulder. "Well, here you are."

Kevin swallowed hard. "Not alone this time."

They found their seats—high up, with a perfect view of the pitch where legends would be made that very afternoon.

The atmosphere was electric, a hum that vibrated in their bones.

As the players emerged—England in white, West Germany in red—the stadium erupted like a living thing.

110,000 voices roared as one.

THE MATCH OF A LIFETIME

The first half was a whirlwind.

THE MEDWAY YEARS

West Germany scored early. The crowd groaned.

Then England equalised shortly after. The stadium thundered. Kevin yelled until his voice cracked. Dougie laughed at him but shouted even louder.

The second half was even more tense. Every pass carried weight. Every tackle drew breaths from 110,000 lungs at once.

When England took the lead, Kevin grabbed Dougie and shook him like a madman.

"We're going to win this!" he shouted.

But then—late heartbreak. A German equaliser with only minutes left. Extra time.

The stadium held its breath.

THE GOAL THAT SHOOK A NATION

Extra time was madness. Then… the moment.

Hurst turned. Shot. The ball hit the crossbar and bounced down. "Is it in?!" Dougie shouted.

"IT'S IN! IT'S IN!" Kevin roared, even before the referee pointed to the centre spot.

The stadium exploded with noise— pure, volcanic, unstoppable joy. Minutes later, Hurst broke free again.

"Some people are on the pitch… they think it's all over—"

And then he scored.

THE MEDWAY YEARS

"It is now!"

Kevin grabbed Dougie in a bear hug, lifting him clean off the ground despite himself. Dougie shouted with laughter. Strangers embraced. Men cried openly. Women danced. Flags whipped in the air like flames. England were World Champions.

And for a moment, the entire country—every street, every town, every soul—felt united, unstoppable, proud.

Leaving the stadium was chaos and magic.

Crowds swarmed the streets. People climbed lampposts, waved banners, sang until they were hoarse.

Kevin and Dougie were swept into Trafalgar Square by the tide of jubilant fans.

Fountains overflowed with people splashing, laughing. Police officers tried to keep order but even they were smiling.

Kevin shouted over the noise, "I can't believe we were there!"

Dougie shouted back, "I can't believe we're alive after all that cheering!"

They found a corner of a pub in Soho, barely big enough for two pints. Someone bought them drinks, then someone else, until they were chatting with Scots, Irishmen, Londoners, even a group of Germans who good-naturedly toasted England's victory.

At some point Kevin leaned back and said, quiet and sincere:

THE MEDWAY YEARS

"This… this is one of the best days of my life."

Dougie nodded. "Mine too, Kev."

"And I wouldn't want to share it with anyone else."

Dougie felt that—deeply. A long, painful chapter between them had finally closed.

On the train back, the sky darkened into deep summer twilight.

Kevin stared out at the blurred countryside, then said softly:

"You know… I'm glad June found you."

Dougie didn't speak at first. Kevin continued.

"You're good for her. You're good… full stop."

Dougie looked at him. "We all get lost sometimes, Kev."

"Not all of us find our way back."

"Yeah," Dougie said quietly. "But some do."

Kevin smiled—a small, peaceful smile. For the first time in years, he felt whole.

When they reached Medway, the streets still buzzed with victory fireworks and drunken singing. June was waiting at the door, Karen in her arms.

"How was it?" she asked.

THE MEDWAY YEARS

Kevin grinned. "Unbelievable."

Dougie stepped toward her, placing a gentle hand on Karen's head.

"I'll tell you everything once she's asleep."

June kissed him softly. "I'll make tea."

Kevin turned to go, hands in his pockets, heart full.

"Kev," June called after him.

He stopped. "I'm glad you two made peace," she said warmly.

Kevin nodded once. "So am I."

Then he walked into the night— not lost, not angry, not broken— but free.

CHAPTER SEVENTEEN – "Paths Across the World"

By 1968, Medway had changed again. New shops. Fresh faces. Recent music in the dance halls—Motown, The Beatles, The Kinks.

But the biggest changes weren't in the streets. They were in the people who once made up the inseparable gang.

THE MEDWAY YEARS

Time had tugged at them all, opening doors they never expected—and closing others they thought would stay open forever.

THE CALL OF DISTANT SHORES

Brian Batchelor stood on the Rochester bridge one warm August morning, hands resting on the cool stone. The river flowed beneath him, slow and deep, carrying secrets out to the estuary.

He'd always been the handsome one. Self-assured. Well-liked.
A natural charmer with the sort of smile that made people imagine bigger futures for him.

But charm didn't pay bills. Not in Medway. Not in 1968.

He'd drifted from job to job—dockyard apprentice, factory shifts, odd repair work—never finding anything that felt like a calling. The world was changing fast: opportunities abroad, money to be made in the oil industry, adventure far beyond Kent.

One evening at The King's Arms, a contractor from Chevron overheard Brian talking about construction work and said quietly:

"You ever think of going someplace hot? Somewhere the money's real? Somewhere men build things that last?"

He placed a brochure on the counter: **Kuwait – Marine & Industrial Construction Opportunities.**

THE MEDWAY YEARS

The images seemed unreal—sparkling seas, giant cranes, sun-bleached sands, men in hard hats standing on enormous steel structures rising from the ocean.

Brian took the brochure home. Read it twice. Then again. That night, something settled in him.

He wanted more. He needed more. The next morning, he posted an application.

MAUREEN – A DIFFERENT KIND OF DUTY

Maureen West stood in her elder sister Eleanor's small bungalow in Waterloo, Ontario, staring at the pale afternoon light spilling across the quilt-covered bed.

Her sister was dying.

Cancer—aggressive, unforgiving—had taken her strength in a matter of months. Eleanor had moved to Canada years earlier after marrying a local teacher, building a family and a life across the ocean. Now those young children—with soft Canadian accents—hovered near the doorway, unsure how to help.

Maureen, once bright and lively in Medway, had grown quiet and drawn since arriving. She spent long hours by Eleanor's bedside, holding her hand, whispering memories only sisters shared.

In England, her letters had grown sporadic. Brian wrote. Barry wrote. Even Brenda wrote from the Navy. But each envelope felt like it belonged to another life.

THE MEDWAY YEARS

Maureen had planned only a short visit. But when the doctor said, *"Your sister needs you now more than ever,"* the decision made itself. She unpacked her case for good. Waterloo became home.

BRIAN'S NEWS

Brian gathered the group—or what was left of it—at a small pub behind Chatham station. It felt strange sitting there: no Tony, now sober but distant; no Brenda, somewhere at sea; no Martin, who was battling his own private struggles; no Maureen.

Just Barry, Dougie, Jackie, and Kevin.

Brian held his pint, swirling it nervously.

"All right," he said finally. "Here it is. I'm leaving Medway."

Barry nearly choked. "You what?"

"I've been offered a contract," Brian said. "Marine construction. Kuwait."

Kevin whistled. "That's miles away."

Dougie raised his glass. "It's a big opportunity, Brian. Proud of you."

Brian smiled appreciatively. "It's good money. Decent work. Something solid."

But beneath the calm tone, something hurt. He'd written to Maureen. Twice. She hadn't replied.

THE MEDWAY YEARS

He didn't know she never even saw the letters—the Canadian postal delays, Eleanor's illness, the chaos of caregiving.

"I thought I'd say goodbye properly," Brian added. "Before I go building harbours in the desert."

Jackie's eyes softened. "We'll miss you. This place won't be the same."

"No," Brian said, "and neither will I. But I'm not going for ever more. I'll get home leave from time to time."

They drank to his future. The mood was proud but tinged with sadness.

Across the ocean, Maureen was spoon-feeding medicine to her sister, unaware that the man she once imagined a future with was preparing to leave her world behind.

Weeks later, Maureen finally found time—time she didn't really have—to write to Dougie and June.

Dear both,

Eleanor is very weak now. The doctors don't sugar-coat things. I'm staying here permanently. She needs me. The children need me. Mother is trying to manage but she's too old to travel this far. I hope everyone is well. I think of home often.
Love, Maureen

June read the letter aloud in the kitchen while stirring porridge for little Karen.

115

THE MEDWAY YEARS

Dougie stood by the window, arms crossed. "She sounds exhausted."

"She is," June said softly. "And she's not coming back."

"Should we write and tell her about Brian?" Dougie asked.

June hesitated. "No. Not yet. Not while she's going through all that."

A WORLD SPLITTING WIDE OPEN

By early winter of '68:

- **Brian boarded a plane at Heathrow**, staring out at the clouds, wondering if Maureen would ever know he left because he wanted more than drifting.

- **Maureen sat in a Canadian hospital room**, holding her sister's hand as snow fell quietly outside.

- **Kevin found work coaching youth football**, calmer, and more patient than he'd ever been.

- **Dougie and June put Karen to bed**, building a small, warm life of their own.

- **Barry married Jackie**, buying a tiny house near Luton Road.

- **Tony reached two years of sobriety**, quietly proud.

- **Martin continued to struggle**, but with Barry's help, he kept going.

THE MEDWAY YEARS

- **Brenda sailed somewhere in the Mediterranean**, sun burning her skin, the world widening beneath her feet.

The late 1960s had scattered them like seeds in the wind each landing in a different soil, growing into different futures.

The gang of Medway had become adults. And none of them were ready for how far from home adulthood sometimes led.

CHAPTER EIGHTEEN – Brian in Kuwait.

Kuwait hit Brian the moment he stepped off the plane— a wall of heat so fierce it felt like opening an oven door.

Not the gentle warmth of an English summer. This was a dry, suffocating blaze that stole breath and pooled sweat in seconds.

He squinted across the tarmac. Endless beige stretched into the horizon—sand, sky, sun. The air shimmered like water over the runways.

"Welcome to hell," a British foreman muttered beside him. Brian choked out a laugh. "Cheerful place, then?"

Although Brian had been briefed that alcoholic drinks were not allowed in Kuwait, he had bought a bottle of Jonnie Walker whisky at Heathrow airport before departure. They even announced on the flight that alcoholic beverages were not allowed in Kuwait.

THE MEDWAY YEARS

But despite this, Brian put the whisky in his hand baggage. But going through customs and immigration it was discovered. The customs officer reprimanded him, and the whisky was confiscated.

A fellow passenger tried to bring in three bottles, and he too was reprimanded and the bottles confiscated.

So, this experience was a clear sign to Brian that he would not be celebrating in pubs and clubs. Kuwait just did not have such establishments. Ah well!

THE WORK

The marine construction site lay along the Persian Gulf— steel skeletons rising from turquoise waters, cranes groaning under the weight of progress.

Construction work can be risky in any part of the world and in Kuwait it was no less risky:

- concrete pouring on half-built jetties,
- welding in stifling heat,
- balancing on narrow beams with waves crashing below.

The heat was relentless. The shifts were long. The danger was constant. He didn't fear it. Sometimes, he welcomed it.

Until 1961 Kuwait had become a protectorate of Great Britain and was now expanding with wealth emanating from huge reserves of crude oil. Although Kuwait formally gained independence in 1961, Iraq initially refused to recognize the

THE MEDWAY YEARS

country's independence by maintaining that Kuwait was part of Iraq.

Kuwait itself had a small population, and most Kuwaitis because of huge oil wealth were supported almost entirely by generous allowances provided by the Kuwait government.

For the rapid expansion and development of the infrastructure, Kuwait was employing people from all over the world to conduct the work.

British, Irish, Egyptian, Indian, Filipino. They shared stories in a blend of languages, hand gestures doing half the talking.

Brian gravitated toward two lads:

Hassan, a Kuwaiti diver with a quiet smile and sharp wit. **Mick**, a rough Irish crane operator who told jokes that made even the foreman blush.

They became his lifeline—friends who asked nothing of him but honesty.

THE NIGHTS

Nights were the hardest. Brian lay awake in his bare, sand-dusted room, ceiling fan clacking as it struggled against the heat. The loneliness crept in then, filling the silence.

He thought of Medway. Of the gang. Of the river. Of Maureen. Especially Maureen.

He had written twice. No reply.

THE MEDWAY YEARS

He told himself it was the post. He told himself she was busy. He told himself he wasn't forgotten.

He didn't believe it.

The Danger

One afternoon, a wave crashed against the jetty at the wrong moment, a surge of water sending two workers slipping toward the edge.

Brian lunged, grabbing one by the shirt, pulling him back to safety as another man caught the second.

Hassan clapped him on the back. "You saved his life."

Brian shrugged. "Just lucky I was at the right place at the time. No more than that. Anyone would have done the same."

But that night, he stared at his shaking hands. For a moment, he wondered if fate had nearly taken him in this far-off land.

He slept badly.

By late '69, Brian understood something painful and true:

He'd left Medway to find himself— but the farther he travelled,
the more fragments of home he carried. Loneliness didn't always mean being alone. Sometimes it meant having too much time to remember.

THE MEDWAY YEARS

CHAPTER NINETEEN – Maureen in Canada.

Waterloo, Ontario was nothing like Medway. The winters were brutal. Snow piled as high as hedges. Ice coated the windows like frosted lace. The local by laws in Canada required homeowners to make sure the pavement was clear at the front of the houses to allow pedestrian traffic free and safe access.

This was a task that Eleanors husband Terry was kept busy with after every snowfall. He had purchased a handheld snow blower for this purpose, which save a lot of time.

Maureen stood in her sister Eleanor's empty bedroom, the smell of lavender still lingering in the air. She pressed a hand to the quilt Eleanor had once stitched. Her sister was gone. And Maureen remained—half caretaker, half lost soul.

THE FUNERAL

THE MEDWAY YEARS

It was small. Quiet. Snow fell softly as if trying to muffle the pain. Eleanor's children clung to Maureen's coat, their breath warm against the icy wind. Maureen had never felt so responsible—or so unsure. Terry and his mother and father along with other family members and friends gathered at the cold graveside. After there were refreshments in the local hotel and for those who could attend.

LEARNING TO STAY

Eleanor's husband Terry, returned to teaching full-time. The children needed meals, routine, comfort. Maureen stepped into the role as if born for it.

She cooked British-style stews in a Canadian kitchen. Helped with schoolwork she barely understood. Laughed when they laughed, cried when they cried.

A community grew around her—neighbours offering casseroles, women from church inviting her for tea, children on the street waving as she passed. She found the Canadians quiet and gentle folks who were so friendly and helpful.

Slowly, she belonged. But grief lingered like a shadow.

Letters She Never Opened

By the time she found Brian's two letters, they were months old, tucked under a pile of unsorted post Eleanor had left on a table. She read them both in one sitting.

Her breath caught.

Kuwait. Construction. Danger. Loneliness. Thinking of you.

THE MEDWAY YEARS

But she was too far. Too numb. Too changed.

She held the letters to her chest and whispered, "I'm sorry," even though no one heard.

A NEW LIFE, QUIETLY MADE

By 1969, Maureen had enrolled in evening classes for office work. She wanted to stand on her own feet, not just Eleanor's memory.

She found she liked Canada—the space, the kindness, the quiet humming of new possibilities. But some nights, staring at the snow outside, she thought of Brian.

And wondered what might have been.

THE MEDWAY YEARS

CHAPTER TWENTY – "Letters Across Oceans"

From 1967 to 1969, the group's lives were scattered across the globe. But envelopes kept them stitched together.

1. KEVIN TO BRIAN (1968)

Mate,
Wembley was the start of me getting my head straight. I'm coaching kids now—turns out I've got patience I never knew I had. Stay safe out there. Bring yourself home in one piece.
K.

2. BRIAN TO KEVIN

Coaching? You? Now I've heard everything. Proud of you, mate.
It's a bloody frying pan here. Miss English rain more than I ever thought.

3. JUNE & DOUGIE TO MAUREEN

Karen can say "Dada" now. She's walking too—straight into everything she shouldn't touch. We miss you. Come home one day, when life is kinder.

THE MEDWAY YEARS

4. MAUREEN TO JUNE

I hold your letters during the hard nights. Karen is beautiful even in photographs. One day, I hope to see her in person. But right now, Canada is where I must be.

5. BRENDA TO BARRY (FROM MALTA)

This place is all sun and sailors. You'd hate it. I love it. Tell Dougie I still have that photo he took. Don't tell him I nearly lost it overboard. Love, B.

6. BRIAN TO MAUREEN (UNSENT DRAFT)

I think of you. Too much. I'll leave it there.

He tore it up.

7. TONY TO DOUGIE (1970)

Three years sober today. Still one day at a time. Met someone. Not sure yet if I deserve her. Hope you're well, mate.

Letters filled the spaces their voices once had. Some were answered. Some lost. Some never posted. But they kept each other alive in memory.

THE MEDWAY YEARS

CHAPTER TWENTY-ONE – Brenda at Sea

Brenda Watson stood on the deck of HMS *Diana*, wind whipping her hair as the destroyer cut through the Mediterranean. She had never imagined this life. Salt spray. The hum of engines. A constant horizon.

1. THE PORTS

Malta, Gibraltar, Crete, Alexandria—each port burst with colour and noise.

Crete smelled of olives and seaweed. Alexandria of spice and diesel. Malta of stone and sunlight.

Brenda tasted foods she couldn't pronounce. Danced with sailors from half the Commonwealth. Wrote postcards she never sent.

2. THE WORK

She wasn't on the front lines—WRNS women rarely were— but she oversaw communications, coordination, codes.

It suited her. Fast-paced. Orderly. Essential. She liked being essential.

3. THE GROWTH

For the first time, Brenda felt **free of Medway**. Free of expectations. Free of being someone's girlfriend or someone's daughter. She learned to rely on herself. And she liked that version of Brenda.

4. THE DISTANCE

But nights were sometimes hard, but not always. She sometimes stared at the moon and wondered where her friends were, what they were doing, whether they'd still recognise her. She missed Dougie's quiet humour. Barry's teasing. June's warmth. But she didn't miss home.

Not yet. She wasn't ready to return.

THE MEDWAY YEARS

CHAPTER TWENTY-TWO– "A New Light"

The church hall smelled of coffee and old wood. Folding chairs were arranged in a circle. On the notice board, a handwritten sign read: FRIDAY NIGHT – AA MEETING – ALL WELCOME

Tony Marks sat two seats away from the door, hands clasped, listening as people shared stories of relapse, redemption, hope. He had spoken many times, but tonight he stayed quiet. He was three years sober. He had a job in a   hardware   shop. He slept through the nights now.

But loneliness lingered. Then she walked in.

THE STRANGER She was in her late twenties, with dark hair tied back, wearing a simple wool coat. Nervous. Trembling faintly as she took a seat opposite Tony.

"Welcome," the group leader said.

She nodded softly. "My name is Sarah. And I… I could use some help."

Her voice was fragile. Honest. Brave. Tony felt something shift inside him.

THE SHARING. She spoke about drinking to ease heartbreak. Tony understood. She spoke about losing herself. Tony understood that too.

When it was his turn, Tony surprised himself.

THE MEDWAY YEARS

"My name is Tony," he said. "And I'm an alcoholic. I used to think I lost everything because of someone else. But I didn't. I lost it because I didn't know how to stay standing."

Sarah looked at him across the circle. Really looked.

And Tony felt seen in a way he hadn't in years.

THE WALK HOME

After the meeting, they left at the same time.

"Are you going home now?" asked Tony.

Sarah replied. "Yes, I live in the flats by Rochester bridge. Not far to walk."

"Please don't think I'm up to something naughty but is it okay if I walk with you?" Tony asked quietly.

Sarah smiled. "I'd like that."

They walked slowly along Rochester High Street, sharing small pieces of their broken histories.

Tony wasn't falling in love. Not yet.

But for the first time in a long, long while— he felt the warmth of possibility.

THE MEDWAY YEARS

CHAPTER TWENTY-THREE – Second Chances

Winter 1970 crept over Medway with quiet certainty—frosted mornings, early sunsets, chimneys breathing pale smoke into the sky. But for Tony Marks, the cold months felt strangely warm for the first time in years. And it had everything to do with Sarah.

They'd met at the AA meeting in November. By December, they walked home together every Friday. By January, Tony found himself checking the clock on Fridays, waiting, hoping, nervous as a teenager again.

He didn't tell anyone. He kept this small light to himself for a while—fearful that naming it too soon might snuff it out.

THE FRIDAY WALK

The ritual began simply.

After the meeting, they left side by side, hands tucked in coat pockets, breath misting the air. The walk from the church hall to Sarah's street wasn't long, but they stretched it out—talking about trivial things, safe things, things that didn't feel heavy.

Her voice was soft, thoughtful. Her laugh was careful at first, then freer.

One evening, she said, "You know… I almost didn't come back at one point during that first meeting."

THE MEDWAY YEARS

Tony looked at her. "What changed your mind?"

"You did," she said. "You stood up and spoke. And you sounded like someone who knew what falling felt like… and what standing again meant."

Tony swallowed hard. "That's all any of us can do. Try to stand again."

Sarah smiled. "You made me believe I could."

The words warmed him inside like a fire.

COFFEE AT THE DOCKSIDE CAFÉ

In late January, Tony finally made a brave move. "Would you… maybe like to get a coffee?" he asked awkwardly after a meeting.

Sarah's eyes brightened. "I'd like that."

They went to the dockside café—one of those places with steamed-up windows, Formica tables, and a jukebox in the corner playing The Seekers. They sat by the window, watching the lights ripple on the dark water.

Sarah stirred her tea slowly. "You're different from most men I've met," she said.

"Different how?"

"You listen. You don't rush. You don't try to pretend you're better than your past."

THE MEDWAY YEARS

Tony stared at his hands. "I'm not proud of it." "You don't have to be proud. Just honest."

He looked up. "I'm trying."

She held his gaze with warmth. "And that's enough."

WHAT TONY WON'T SAY

There were things Tony didn't talk about very often Maggie. The drinking. The nights sleeping rough. The shame that had carved valleys in him.

But one evening, as they walked past the old Riverview Hall—now used only occasionally for events—Sarah paused.

"You came here often?" she asked.

Tony nodded. "Too often."

He stared up at the building, remembering the bright lights, the laughter, the moments that had led to his downfall.

"I was someone else then," he murmured. "Someone I don't want to be again."

Sarah touched his sleeve lightly. "Then you're not. You're who you are now. That's what matters."

Her touch was gentle—but it steadied him.

THE MEDWAY YEARS

THE DINNER THAT ALMOST DIDN'T HAPPEN

In February, Tony invited her to dinner at a small Italian place in Rochester.

He shaved. Pressed his shirt. Nearly talked himself out of it twice.

Sarah arrived wearing a navy dress and a shy smile. "You look lovely," Tony managed.

"You look terrified," she teased.

"I am."

They both laughed, tension melting. Dinner was comfortable stories exchanged across the table, slow smiles, the kind of pauses that don't feel awkward because they're shared.

But halfway through dessert, the waiter poured wine at a nearby table. The sharp scent filled the air.

Tony's throat tightened instantly. His hands trembled slightly.

Sarah noticed. "You all right?"

Tony looked at the wine, then at her.

"I'm fine," he said quietly. "I just… I still get moments."

Sarah nodded, reaching across the table.

" So do I occasionally. But we're allowed moments, Tony. We're human."

He breathed out slowly. The tightness eased.

THE MEDWAY YEARS

For the first time, Tony felt like someone was sitting *with* him—not judging, not pitying, just understanding.

THE FIRST TOUCH

One cold March evening, as Tony walked Sarah home, snowflakes drifting down in lazy spirals, she slipped slightly on an icy patch.

Tony instinctively caught her arm.

Her hand stayed on his arm a moment longer than necessary.

She looked up at him; cheeks flushed from cold or something warmer.

"Thank you," she whispered.

"For what?"

"For being steady."

Tony swallowed, heart thudding. "I'm trying."

Sarah took his hand—tentative, gentle.

"You're succeeding," she said.

And they walked the rest of the way hand in hand.

THE MEDWAY YEARS

THE FEAR OF HAPPINESS

Tony lay awake that night, staring at the ceiling, terrified. He'd ruined things before. He'd fallen apart. Broken hearts—including his own.

He feared hurting Sarah. Scared of letting her down. Scared of being happy. But he also knew something else: For the first time in years, he *wanted* a future. Not just sobriety.
Not just survival. A life. With someone.

With her.

HER LETTER

One week later, Sarah handed him a small envelope.

"Only read it when you're home," she said.

Tony nodded, heart racing. At home, he sat at his small kitchen table and opened it carefully. Inside:

Tony,
I know you're afraid. I am too. But fear isn't a warning—it's a sign we care about something deeply. I don't want perfection. I don't want promises you can't keep. I just want to walk beside you, one day at a time. If that's too much, tell me. If it's not enough, tell me that too.

Yours,
Sarah

Tony folded the letter, hands trembling.

THE MEDWAY YEARS

He realised then— this was not just affection. Not convenience. Not loneliness finding company. This was the beginning of something real. Something steady. Patient. Possible. Something he thought he was done deserving.

But maybe he wasn't.

THE DECISION

At the next meeting, when everyone was packing their chairs away, Tony approached her.

He held her letter. "I want that," he said. "What you wrote. One day at a time. With you."

Sarah's eyes softened. "Then that's what we'll have."

She laced her fingers with his. Not tight. Not claiming.

Just warm.

And Tony felt, for the first time in years, that the future wasn't something to fear— but something he could walk toward.

With someone watching the road beside him.

CHAPTER TWENTY-FOUR – "New Roads, Old Friends"

By the spring of 1971, Tony Marks had settled into something he never imagined he would have again: routine,

THE MEDWAY YEARS

stability, gentle happiness. The kind that didn't rush him, didn't overwhelm him, didn't threaten to slip through his fingers when he wasn't looking.

And that happiness had a name:

Sarah.

BRIGHTON: FIRST TRIP

They chose Brighton for their first weekend away. Not far. Not extravagant. Safe. Simple. Exactly what Tony needed.

Sarah stepped off the train in a pale blue coat, her eyes lighting up at the sight of the sea stretching beyond the promenade.

"It's beautiful," she said.

Tony smiled. "Wait until you hear the seagulls steal your chips. That's the real Brighton experience."

She laughed—a soft, musical sound that eased the tension in his shoulders.

THE PIER

They walked the pier hand in hand, stopping for doughnuts, watching children race each other, fishermen hunched against the railings. Tony bought Sarah a small silver charm from a kiosk—a tiny anchor.

"A reminder of steadiness," he said awkwardly.

She touched his arm gently. "And of the sea bringing things together."

THE MEDWAY YEARS

They sat at the end of the pier, letting the wind ruffle their hair.

"This feels right," Sarah whispered. Tony nodded. "It does." And for once, he wasn't afraid to agree.

A PEACEFUL EVENING

They stayed at a modest guesthouse near the seafront. Two single rooms—Tony wanted to take things slow, respectfully.

After dinner, they walked along the shingle beach as dusk settled, the lights across the water flickering like scattered stars. Tony stopped suddenly. "Sarah... can I say something daft?"

She turned, smiling. "You can say anything."

"I feel... safe with you."

Sarah's expression softened. "That isn't daft. That's beautiful."

And when she kissed him—slow, gentle, certain—Tony realised he wasn't just building a new life.

He was building a future.

PART II — "MEET THE BARNES FAMILY"

Two weeks later, Sarah met Dougie and June.

Tony had worried for days. Would they approve? Would they see how fragile and precious this new happiness was? Would they judge him for the man he used to be?

THE MEDWAY YEARS

He paced the pavement outside Dougie's house until Sarah threaded her arm through his.

"Stop worrying," she whispered. "They're your friends."

Tony swallowed. "Yes. They are."

June opened the door, smiling warmly. "You must be Sarah! Come in, love."

The house was full of familiar sounds—kettle boiling, Karen's laughter drifting from upstairs, the smell of Sunday roast clinging to the walls.

Sarah looked around with soft admiration. "It's lovely," she said.

"Not as lovely as having you here," June replied.

Dougie shook Tony's hand, then Sarah's. "Anyone who makes Tony smile like that is a friend of ours."

Tony flushed crimson. "Dougie…"

But Sarah squeezed his hand proudly.

1. Tea and Stories

They sat around the kitchen table—tea, biscuits, Karen's excited chatter, June's warm energy filling every corner.

Sarah talked about her work, her childhood, her own struggles. She didn't hide her past.

June respected that immediately. Dougie too.

At one point, Karen climbed onto Tony's knee and asked, "Is she your girlfriend?" Tony froze, embarrassed.

THE MEDWAY YEARS

Sarah laughed gently. "Something like that."

Dougie grinned. "Nice to see you glowing, mate." Tony ducked his head. "I feel different. Better."

June touched his arm. "You deserve better."

Sarah slipped her hand into his under the table. He didn't pull away.

"KEVIN SEES THE CHANGE"

Later that evening, Tony bumped into Kevin near the old dance hall—Kevin carrying a kit bag after youth football practice.

"Tony," Kevin called. "Heard you were bringing someone to meet the Barnes family today."

Tony rubbed the back of his neck. "Yeah. Sarah. We're… seeing each other."

Kevin smiled—genuine, warm. "No surprise there. You look different."

"Different?"

"Lighter. Like someone took a weight off your spine."

Tony shrugged awkwardly. "I'm trying."

Kevin nodded, leaning on the railing. "And succeeding, mate. I can always spot a man fighting his demons—did it myself long enough."

THE MEDWAY YEARS

Tony met his eyes. There was no judgement. Only understanding. "Thanks, Kev," Tony said quietly. "Means a lot."

Kevin clapped him on the shoulder. "You keep hold of that girl. And keep hold of yourself while you're at it. You've worked bloody hard."

Tony felt a surge of gratitude. Kevin wasn't just proud—he was relieved.

It felt like a full circle moment: two men once broken, now rebuilt.

THE EVENING ENDING

When Tony walked Sarah home later, she slipped her arm into his. "Your friends are lovely," she said.

"They're my family," Tony replied.

"And what am I?" she teased softly.

Tony stopped walking. Looked at her seriously.

"You're the best thing that's happened to me in years."

Sarah's eyes warmed. "And you're the kindest man I've ever met."

He shook his head. "No. I've just finally learned how to be the man I should've been."

Sarah touched his cheek gently. "I think you're becoming the man you were always meant to be."

THE MEDWAY YEARS

They kissed under the streetlamp— warm, slow, hopeful.

The kind of kiss that told Tony:

He wasn't just surviving anymore. He wasn't just sober. He was living. And he was ready for whatever the future held.

CHAPTER TWENTY-FIVE – "A Promise Made Slowly"

Medway in 1975 was changing again—more cars on the streets, new estates being built, young families pushing prams along High Street. But for Tony Marks, the biggest changes were quieter, unfolding in the everyday moments he shared with Sarah.

Their love was not fireworks. It wasn't the dramatic rush he'd once known in younger years. It was a warm lamp lit in a small room—steady, lasting, soft.

After four years together, people had begun asking when he'd "get on with it." But Tony refused to be rushed. He wanted to be sure—sure he was strong enough, sure he was ready, sure he would never again be the man he used to be.

Sarah never pushed. She never hinted. She simply *was*, beside him, day after day. And that was why Tony loved her even more.

A Day Like Any Other

THE MEDWAY YEARS

It was late September, crisp and gold, the kind of day when the leaves along the Rochester Esplanade rustled like soft applause. Tony and Sarah took their usual Saturday walk, arm in arm, watching children kick footballs across the grass.

Sarah pointed to the river. "Looks peaceful today."

Tony nodded. "Almost makes you forget it ever floods."

She laughed softly—her laugh still made his chest warm after all these years.

They walked slowly, not speaking much. That was the comfort of their love—words weren't needed to fill the space.

But inside Tony's coat pocket, his fingers kept brushing the small velvet box he'd been carrying since morning.

His heart thudded every time.

He'd planned a moment, a speech, something meaningful. But now, walking beside her, he felt the tightness in his chest. The weight of what he was about to offer. The enormity of it.

Am I ready? Am I enough?

Sarah looked up at him. "You're quiet today."

"Just thinking," he said.

"About anything good?"

"About everything good," he murmured, squeezing her hand.

THE BENCH BY THE WATER

THE MEDWAY YEARS

They reached an old wooden bench overlooking the river—a place they often rested. Tony tapped the seat gently. "Sit?"

"Of course."

She sat gracefully, smoothing her skirt. Tony sat beside her, palms sweating.

He looked at her for a long moment, taking in the familiar lines of her face, the gentle strength in her eyes, the way the wind played with her hair.

"Sarah," he began, voice low, "do you ever think about… the future?"

She turned toward him, curiosity softening her features. "I do," she said. "Sometimes I imagine where we'll be in ten years. Close to here, I hope."

"You think about us?"

"Of course I do."

That answer steadied him.

"Do you remember," Tony said quietly, "the first thing I ever said to you?"

She smiled. "That you were trying to stand again."

Tony nodded. "And you said you believed I could."

"I still do."

The tension in his chest loosened—just a little.

He took a slow breath. "Sarah… you've walked with me through every step of my rebuilding. You didn't try to fix me.

THE MEDWAY YEARS

You didn't try to drag me forward. You just held my hand when I needed it."

Sarah's eyes glistened. "You help me stand too," she whispered.

That settled it.

THE RING

Tony's heart hammered as he reached into his coat and pulled out the small velvet box. Sarah inhaled sharply but didn't speak.

"I'm not a perfect man," Tony began slowly. "And I never will be. The past... it's still part of me. But I've learned something these last years—that love doesn't ask for perfection. Just honesty. Effort. And two people willing to walk side by side."

He opened the box.

Inside was a simple gold ring—no diamonds, no unnecessary flourish. Just warm, understated beauty. Like Sarah.

Sarah pressed a hand to her mouth.

Tony took the ring, his fingers trembling.

THE MEDWAY YEARS

"I can't promise I'll never stumble," he said. "But I can promise I'll always stand back up—and I want to stand with you. For the rest of my life."

He swallowed hard. "Sarah… will you marry me?"

For a moment, she didn't move. Didn't breathe.

Then tears spilled quietly down her cheeks.

"Yes," she whispered. "Yes, Tony. A thousand times yes."

Tony exhaled deeply—like letting go of years of fear in a single breath.

He slipped the ring onto her finger. Sarah threw her arms around him, holding him with both joy and certainty.

And for the first time in years, Tony felt something he never expected to feel again— **whole.**

AFTER THE YES

They walked home slowly, fingers tightly intertwined.

No fanfare. No cheering crowds. Just the quiet joy of two people choosing each other carefully, gently.

When they reached Sarah's doorstep, she stood on tiptoes and whispered:

"I always knew we were going somewhere. I just didn't know when you'd be brave enough to ask."

Tony laughed softly. "I've never been brave. I've just been lucky."

THE MEDWAY YEARS

"Not lucky," Sarah said firmly. "Worth it."

He held her close, warmed from the inside out.

And somewhere inside him, the boy who once lost himself entirely realised the truth— He'd finally found his place in the world. And it was right beside her.

CHAPTER TWENTY-SIX — "Forty Years and Change"

Medway in 1980 wasn't the Medway of 1961. The terraces looked smaller somehow, as if the years had pressed down on them. The dockyard—once the beating heart of work, noise, and pride—stood partly derelict now, rumours of closure spreading like winter fog.

But the souls who'd grown up there—the boys and girls who'd danced, fought, loved, and broken together—were still connected by something invisible but undeniable.

They were older. Softer in some places, harder in others. Lives had taken them in different directions, but as the seventies gave way to the eighties, a tug pulled many of them back toward one another, toward home, toward meaning.

It began quietly. A letter. A wedding anniversary. A return visit.
The changing of seasons in their own lives.

THE MEDWAY YEARS

And suddenly, without planning to, they all found themselves drifting back into each other's orbit.

CHAPTER TWENTY-SEVEN — "Dougie & June: A Life in Full"

Dougie Barnes stood outside his small semi-detached house in Rainham, wiping oil from his hands after another Saturday morning working on the ageing Cortina. The air smelled faintly of cut grass, petrol, and the promise of spring.

Behind him, from inside the house, he could hear laughter— June and their sixteen-year-old daughter Karen arguing light-heartedly about hairstyles, school discos, and the latest fashion trends.

Life had been kind to Dougie. Not perfect—there had been money worries, job uncertainty, and the usual trials of raising a daughter—but *kind*.

June stepped out onto the doorstep, holding two mugs of tea.

"You're getting too old to crawl under cars," she teased.

"And you're getting too bossy to ignore," he replied, kissing her cheek.

Karen poked her head out the door. "Dad, are you taking me into town later? I've got to buy a birthday present for Suzy."

Dougie pretended to think. "Hm... depends. Have you done your homework?"

THE MEDWAY YEARS

Karen groaned theatrically. "You two should've been *comedians.*"

She retreated inside with a laugh, the slam of her bedroom door punctuating her teenage exasperation.

June and Dougie stood side by side in easy silence, sipping tea.

"You ever think," June began softly, "what life would've been like if things had gone differently? Back then, I mean?"

Dougie thought of Kevin. Tony. Barry. Brenda. Brian. Maureen. Martin.

Then he shook his head.

"No," he said. "This is the life I was supposed to have."

June leaned her head on his shoulder. "I think so too."

CHAPTER TWENTY-EIGHT — "Tony & Sarah: The Long Road to Peace"

Tony Marks was a changed man, though he still carried pieces of his past the way old soldiers carry shrapnel— quietly, privately.

He and Sarah lived in a modest house in Chatham, one decorated with warm colours, knitted throws, bookshelves, and the sense of calm that had taken them both years to build.

THE MEDWAY YEARS

Tony now managed the hardware shop where he'd once been just another struggling employee. His boss had retired and trusted Tony with the whole operation, even the books— something unthinkable twenty years earlier.

On a Saturday in March 1980, Tony stood behind the counter, reorganising display shelves while Sarah added new stock behind him.

"You're fussing," she said gently.

"I'm not," Tony replied. "You are. When you fuss, it means you're thinking too much."

He sighed. "You know me too well."

"Better than you know yourself."

He set down the hammer he was holding. "You remember I mentioned the AA anniversary?"

Sarah nodded. "Ten years, isn't it?"

"Ten years today."

She crossed the shop floor and took his hand with a softness that still startled him. "I'm proud of you," she whispered.

"I'm proud of us," he replied.

They closed the shop early that afternoon and walked to the meeting hall together, hand in hand, sunlight warming their steps.

The man who once lived in doorways now stood straight, steady, loved, and loving.

THE MEDWAY YEARS

Tony never forgot where he'd been. But he finally knew where he belonged.

CHAPTER TWENTY-NINE — "Kevin: A Coach, A Father, A Man Redeemed"

The football pitch behind the old primary school was overgrown but serviceable. Kevin Powers stood at the centre circle, whistle dangling around his neck, watching a group of teenagers attempting dribbling drills with varying degrees of success—and enthusiasm.

"Come on, lads!" Kevin shouted. "If you want to play properly on Saturday, you need to learn to pass *before* you lose the ball, not after!"

A skinny boy with oversized boots shouted back, "Then stop picking me for left wing, coach!"

Kevin laughed—a rich, easy laugh he hadn't known in his twenties.

Training wrapped at four. By half-past, Kevin was walking home to a small, terraced house where his wife, Pamela, waited for him.

He'd met her in 1973—kind, honest, patient. She didn't know the boy he'd once been, she only knew the man he'd worked hard to become.

As he pushed open the door, their young son, Danny, ran at him full speed.

THE MEDWAY YEARS

"Dad! Dad! I scored at practice today!"

Kevin scooped him up and spun him around. "Of course you did!"

Later, after dinner, he sat alone in the garden, letting the cool air settle on his skin. He thought of June sometimes, but not painfully. He thought of the dance hall, the shadows of who he'd been, the fire in his chest that once consumed everything.

- But life had changed him.
- Fatherhood had softened him.
- Coaching had grounded him.
- Pamela had steadied him. And forgiveness—from himself, and from Dougie—had set him free.

CHAPTER THIRTY— "Barry & Jackie: The Quiet Hearth"

Barry Medhurst never liked fuss or drama. He preferred steady seasons, steady work, steady home life. By 1980 he had all three.

He and Jackie lived in a semi-detached in Wigmore, two children—Paul and Alison—already towering toward teenage years.

Barry now worked as a foreman on a construction crew. Jackie worked part-time in a local shop. Their life wasn't glamorous. But it was full.

THE MEDWAY YEARS

One evening, as the kids bickered over the television channel, Jackie sat beside Barry on the sofa and nudged him.

"You ever hear from the others?" she asked softly.

"Now and then. Tony mostly."

"And Dougie?"

"He's doing well. Always did have a good head on him."

Jackie nodded. "I think we were lucky, you know."

"How d'you mean?"

"We grew up. Settled down. Made it work. Some people never do."

Barry put an arm around her. "Yeah. Guess we're not doing too badly."

CHAPTER THIRTY-ONE — "Brenda: Return from the Sea"

Brenda Watson stepped off the train at Chatham station wearing a navy-blue blazer, her WRNS badge pinned to the lapel. Her hair was shorter now, peppered with grey despite her forty-two years. Service life had done that to her—sun, discipline, distance, and pride.

She'd returned to Medway for the first time in almost a decade.

Walking through town felt surreal. Shops had changed. Roads widened. Faces younger.

THE MEDWAY YEARS

She wondered if the others would recognise her. She wondered if she would recognise herself.

Back in 1963 she'd fled Medway, thinking it was the only way to become something other than a girl trapped by expectations.

Now she returned a woman forged by oceans.

Her first stop was always going to be the Barnes house.

CHAPTER THIRTY-TWO— "Brian: The Long Journey Home"

Brian Batchelor stood inside Heathrow Airport, case in hand, waiting for the train that would take him back to Medway.

His hair was greyer now, his skin darkened by decades under desert suns. His eyes were wiser, steadier. He'd spent nearly twenty years working abroad—Kuwait, Bahrain, Qatar—building harbours, oil terminals, and breakwaters.

His body carried the wear of it—scars, stiff joints, a slight limp from a fall in '74.

But the largest mark was inside him.

He'd thought often of Maureen. Too often.

He knew she was in Canada still. He knew she might never return. He wasn't sure why 1980 felt like the year he needed to come home, but something in him said it was time.

THE MEDWAY YEARS

Time to revisit where he'd begun. Time to face the past he'd outrun.

Time to see what remained.

CHAPTER THIRTY-THREE— "Maureen: Another Winter in Canada"

Maureen West watched snow gather on the windowsill of her small house in Waterloo, Ontario. She'd stayed after Eleanor died. She'd built a life. Worked as a school office administrator. Helped raise her nieces and nephews. Became part of the community.

Though Medway was still inside her—an ache in quiet hours—this was her home now. She'd loved only once, really. And she'd never told Brian that.

One evening, after clearing away supper dishes, she opened a tin box where she kept keepsakes—photographs, letters, plane tickets, scraps of home.

Inside lay two letters from Brian. Still folded. Still precious. Still painful. She pressed them to her chest.

"He's part of another life," she whispered to the quiet room. "Not this one."

And yet, some nights she dreamed of him.

THE MEDWAY YEARS

CHAPTER THIRTY-FOUR — "Threads Drawn Together"

In late spring, by coincidence—or something like fate—a pattern began forming.

Brenda returned home. Brian returned home. Tony celebrated ten years sober. Kevin's team prepared for a local final. Dougie and June's anniversary approached. Barry and Jackie planned a summer gathering.

One by one, like moths circling back toward a familiar flame, the old group found themselves reconnecting… slowly at first, then with growing warmth.

Phone calls. Letters. Unexpected knocks on doors.

By July 1980, the gang—scattered across continents, decades, heartbreaks, and triumphs—were on the brink of seeing each other again.

And none of them knew how profound that reunion would be.

CHAPTER THIRTY-FIVE – "Plans in the Air"

It started with a simple idea over a cup of tea.

Barry and Jackie sat at their kitchen table one evening in May 1980, bills and school letters pushed to one side, space cleared for something more pleasant.

"You know what we haven't done in years?" Jackie said, stirring her tea.

"Had any peace and quiet," Barry replied.

THE MEDWAY YEARS

She nudged him with her foot. "No, silly. I mean all of us. The old gang. Properly. Not just bumping into each other."

Barry leaned back, thinking. "We're all scattered now."

"But not that far," Jackie said. "Well—" she paused, thinking of Canada and the Gulf. "Most of us."

Barry scratched his chin. "You thinking what I'm thinking?"

"Garden party," Jackie said, eyes lighting up. "Summer. Here. We've got the space. Everyone brings a bit of food. We've got enough chairs, and we can borrow from next door."

Barry smiled slowly. "We could. You really want to see them all again?"

She nodded. "We're all getting older, Baz. You think we'll always have time but look how fast it goes."

He thought of Kevin, calm and older now; of Tony with his quiet smile; of Dougie and June; of Brenda, back from the sea; of Brian, somewhere in the Middle East; of Martin, drifting on the edges.

"All right," he said. "Let's do it."

Jackie pulled a notepad closer. "Right then. We'll write to…"

And one by one, she began to list the names that had once meant an entire world.

THE MEDWAY YEARS

CHAPTER THIRTY-SIX – "Gathering"

It was a warm Saturday in July when Barry and Jackie's back garden became a meeting place for the past.

The washing line had been taken down. Folding chairs circled around a couple of trestle tables laden with sausage rolls, sandwiches, quiches, crisps, and Jackie's famous trifle. Kids darted about like bright little comets, trailing laughter and shouts.

The first to arrive were Dougie, June, and Karen. Karen, now sixteen, towered between her parents, all long limbs and impatience.

"Blimey," Barry said as they came through the side gate. "She's not the little tot that used to steal biscuits anymore."

"She'll still steal biscuits," Dougie said. "She's just quicker now."

Karen rolled her eyes. "Hello, Uncle Barry. Auntie Jackie." She hugged Jackie, awkward but sincere. "It smells lovely out here."

"Wait till you taste it," Jackie said. "Go say hello to the trifle, make friends."

Next came Kevin with Pamela and young Danny, who already had a football under his arm.

"Couldn't leave it at home, could you?" Kevin said, ruffling his son's hair.

"What if someone wants a kickabout?" Danny protested.

THE MEDWAY YEARS

"We'll move the breakables," Barry muttered.

Tony and Sarah arrived soon after, bearing a homemade sponge cake. Tony's shoulders straightened the moment he saw the familiar faces, nerves loosening in the warmth of their welcome.

"Well, look at us," he said, smiling. "Who'd have thought we'd all last this long?"

"Speak for yourself," Kevin replied. "I still feel twenty-one."

"Your knees would disagree," Dougie said.

Laughter rippled around them like the old days, but softer now. Gentler. No longer desperate to prove something—just relieved to be there.

Brenda appeared at the gate a little later, in a simple summer dress, her posture straight from years of service, her eyes bright and wary. "Permission to come aboard?" she called.

"Always," Dougie said, already moving to hug her.

"Brenda!" June wrapped her up in a tight embrace. "Look at you. Proper officer and everything."

"Retired now," Brenda said. "Or at least on shore long enough to remember where home is."

"You back for good?" Jackie asked.

Brenda hesitated. "For a while. We'll see where the wind blows."

"And we're straight back to boat metaphors," Kevin said. "Some things never change."

THE MEDWAY YEARS

They were all there now. Almost.

Two gaps remained in the circle of old names. Brian. And Maureen.

CHAPTER THIRTY-SEVEN – "Brian Returns"

The afternoon sun was sliding lower when the side gate creaked again. Barry looked up from the barbecue, smoke curling around his head.

A man in his early forties stepped through, carrying a bottle of wine awkwardly, as if not sure it was enough.

His hair was flecked with grey. His skin weathered and tanned.
His eyes older, but still recognisable. "Brian," Dougie said quietly.

Conversation faltered. Heads turned. For a moment, time folded back twenty years.

"Hello, lads," Brian said, voice rougher but warm. "Ladies. Anyone still speaking to me?"

It broke the tension. Laughter and shouts erupted.

"Get over here, you idiot," Kevin said, grabbing him in a hug.

One by one, they embraced him—Barry, Tony, Brenda, June. Even Karen, who'd only heard stories.

"Uncle Brian," she said cautiously.

THE MEDWAY YEARS

"Blimey, you make us feel ancient," Brian replied.

He soon found himself with a plate in hand. As he settled into a chair, Dougie sat beside him.

"How long you back for?" Dougie asked.

"Dunno yet," Brian said. "Job finished. Might take another abroad. Might not. Thought I'd better remember what English rain feels like before I decide."

They shared a quiet chuckle.

"Have you heard from…?" Brian began, then stopped.

"Maureen?" Dougie finished.

Brian nodded.

"A letter now and then," Dougie said. "She's in Canada. Still. Doesn't say much about herself. Always asks after everyone."

Brian looked down at his food. "Right."

"You should write," Dougie said softly.

"I did," Brian replied. " Long time ago. Don't know if it was the right thing," The sounds of chatter and children playing floated over them.

"Funny, isn't it?" Brian continued. "We went half-way around the world, and here we are back in a garden in Medway, acting like we never left."

"We didn't," Dougie said quietly. "Not really."

Their conversation was interrupted by a call from Jackie.

THE MEDWAY YEARS

"Pictures!" she cried, holding an old Polaroid camera. "Before everyone gets greasy and sweaty and full of trifle."

They gathered together, arms slung around shoulders, kids squashed in front. For a moment, as the camera clicked, the years blurred completely.

A slice of youth, captured in middle age.

CHAPTER THIRTY-EIGHT– "A Knock at the Gate"

The sun was beginning to lower into a hazy gold when it happened. The side gate creaked for the last time that day.

Jackie, carrying a tray of empty glasses, glanced up.

A woman stood uncertainly just inside the gate, hand still on the latch.

She was older now—fine lines around her eyes, hair darker and tied back, dressed neatly but simply. There was something Canadian about her now in the cut of her coat, the shape of her posture.

But her eyes were pure Medway. "Maureen?" Jackie breathed.

The tray tilted dangerously. Brenda darted forward to take it.

Maureen smiled, small and unsure. "Hello, Jack. Hope I'm not too late."

THE MEDWAY YEARS

For a heartbeat, no one moved. Then June was there, arms around her, pulling her close.

"Reenie," she whispered. "Reenie, love."

Maureen clung back, shoulders shaking like someone who hadn't quite believed they'd really done this—really come home.

"I wasn't sure I'd be welcome," she murmured.

"Don't be daft," Barry said, voice thick. "You didn't think we'd leave you in Canada forever, did you?"

They surrounded her: Jackie, Kevin, Tony, Dougie, Brenda, even the teenagers hovering with nervous curiosity.

Then, a fraction later than the others, Brian approached.

He held himself back for a second, standing just at the edge of the circle.

Maureen lifted her head.

Their eyes met.

And the garden fell away.

CHAPTER THIRTY-NINE– "Maureen & Brian"

The noise of the party became a distant murmur. Chairs, children, smoke, glasses—all of it blurred.

THE MEDWAY YEARS

For a moment, they were back in 1961—two young people at a dance, the air thick with cigarette smoke and music, hearts full of possibility.

"Hello, Maureen," Brian said softly.

"Hello, Brian."

He hadn't heard her say his name in nearly twenty years.

"You look well," he said, because it was all he could think to say that didn't sound like *I've missed you every day.*

"So do you," she replied, even though he looked tired, older, and different. Or maybe because he did.

Someone—sensible, kind—nudged them gently toward the quieter end of the garden, near the fence where the bushes gave a little privacy.

"You didn't tell us you were coming," Brian managed.

"I wasn't sure I would," Maureen said. "I came over because… well. Mum passed in the spring. I had to come for the estate, lawyers, all the rest of it. June wrote about this get-together. I almost didn't come."

"Why?"

"Because I wasn't sure I could see you," she said honestly. "And then I wasn't sure I could *not* see you. In the end I flipped a coin."

"Which side was I on?" Brian asked quietly.

She smiled. "Both."

THE MEDWAY YEARS

He laughed—short and breathless.

They stood in silence for a moment, the noise of the others floating over the lawn like a softer echo of what they once were.

"I wrote to you, you know," he said. "Back then. From Kuwait."

"I know," she replied.

His eyes widened. "You got them?"

"Not at the time," Maureen said. "Eleanor was terribly ill. The house was chaotic. I found your letters months later under a pile of papers." She looked down. "By then… everything felt too late to answer."

Brian swallowed hard. "I thought you'd just… moved on."

"I hadn't," she said quietly. "I just moved. There's a difference."

He nodded slowly.

"I kept them," she added. "Your letters. I still have them."

A breeze stirred the leaves along the fence. The scent of charcoal and summer grass drifted around them.

"You ever…?" He stopped, unsure if he wanted the answer.

"Move on?" she finished gently. "I built a life. A good one. Work. Friends. The children needed me after Eleanor died. I became part of things. I've been… content, most of the time."

"And the rest?" he asked.

THE MEDWAY YEARS

She looked at him, eyes shining.

"The rest of the time I wondered where you were," she said. "Whether you were happy. Whether you'd married some dazzling woman with perfect hair and a sensible pension."

He flashed a rueful grin. "Afraid not. Never quite got round to it."

"Never?"

"Never," he said simply. "Always felt like I'd left something unfinished. Hard to start something new when you think you haven't put the last chapter to bed properly."

Their eyes held.

"Brian," she said softly. "We were stupid, you know. Back then."

"Hopeless," he agreed. "Thought there was always more time."

"We didn't know better," she said.

"We do now," he replied.

A burst of laughter from the table made them glance back: Kevin showing a trick, Tony shaking his head, children dodging around them.

"Our lives are... different now," Maureen said, turning back. "We can't just pick up where we left off. That place doesn't exist anymore."

"I know," Brian said. "We're not those people."

THE MEDWAY YEARS

"But" she added, voice barely above a whisper, "I don't think what I felt for you ever really left. It just… went quiet for a while."

Brian's breath left him, like someone had pressed a hand to his chest and squeezed.

"Same here," he admitted. "Sometimes I'd be on a breakwater halfway to nowhere, and I'd think about you standing by the old school gates as if I'd see you again if I looked hard enough."

She laughed, tears in her eyes. "Daft."

"Completely."

They stood in silence, letting the truth settle between them— not sharp, not accusing. Just honest. "What now then?" he asked quietly.

"I don't know," she said. "I go back to Canada, at least for a while. My life is there. Your roots are here. We've both got responsibilities, connections."

"Doesn't have to be all or nothing," he said slowly. "There are letters. There are phones. There's… visits."

She watched him carefully. "You'd want that?"

"Yes," he said, no hesitation now. "I would."

She let out a breath that sounded suspiciously like relief.

"Then maybe," Maureen said, "this doesn't have to be an ending."

"Maybe it's a late start," he replied.

THE MEDWAY YEARS

"We're getting old for new starts," she teased.

"Maybe," he said. "Or maybe now's exactly when we know enough to get it right."

She smiled—properly now, the way she hadn't smiled in years.

"Give me your address," she said. "The proper one. And this time, if you write, I'll answer."

He reached into his pocket for a pen, hands trembling only slightly.

Behind them, Dougie glanced over—saw them standing a little apart, talking quietly, their faces soft and open.

June came to stand beside him.

"Look at them," she whispered.

"Think they've still got it?" Dougie asked.

"It never really went," June replied. "It just needed permission to come back."

CHAPTER FORTY – "Old Stories, New Truths"

As the evening slipped into gold and then into the soft blue of early night, the party settled into the kind of comfortable rhythm only shared history can hold.

THE MEDWAY YEARS

At one of the tables, Tony leaned back, listening to Kevin recount a story about a disastrous youth match where three of his players had forgotten which goal was theirs.

"So, you won 3–2?" Tony asked.

"We lost 2–1," Kevin said. "Own goals. You couldn't make it up."

Sarah and Pamela laughed. "So, you still love it?" Sarah asked Kevin.

"More than I ever loved playing," Kevin said. "These kids— half of them don't have fathers who show up. I get to be that for ninety minutes on a Saturday. That's enough for me."

At another corner, Brenda sat beside Martin, who'd arrived late and hovered at the fringes before she hauled him into a chair.

He looked thin but cleaner than she remembered, eyes tired but steady.

"How's life treating you, Mart?" she asked.

"Gently, for a change," he said. "Odd jobs. Bit of painting. Landlord hasn't thrown me out yet."

"You'd tell us if you were struggling?" she pressed.

"Maybe," he said. "More likely I'd hide and hope someone comes knocking."

She squeezed his shoulder. "Then expect frequent knocks."

Near the back door, Dougie and Tony leaned against the wall, watching the others.

THE MEDWAY YEARS

"Funny, isn't it?" Tony said. "We thought everything finished when we were twenty."

"We were idiots," Dougie replied.

"Speak for yourself."

"I *am* speaking for you," Dougie said. They shared a grin. "Do you ever wish you could go back?" Tony asked after a moment.

"Sometimes," Dougie said. "But only if I could take what I know now with me."

"What would you change?"

Dougie watched Karen chatting to Danny and the other kids. June laughing with Jackie. Kevin ruffling his son's hair. Brenda listening to Martin. Brian and Maureen still in the corner, still talking.

"Honestly?" Dougie said. "Not much. We got hurt. We made mistakes. But we all ended up… here."

Tony nodded. "Together. In some shape or form."

"That's more than a lot of people get," Dougie said.

CHAPTER FORTY-ONE – "Last Light"

As the party thinned, people drifting away with hugs and promises to "not leave it so long next time," the sky turned indigo.

Kevin and his family left first, Danny protesting that the night was "still young," despite yawning.

THE MEDWAY YEARS

Brenda stayed later, washing dishes with Jackie, sleeves rolled up, laughing about incompetent sailors and stubborn officers.

Martin slipped away quietly after making eye contact with Barry, who gave a subtle nod that said, *I see you. I'll check on you later.*

Tony and Sarah walked home arm in arm, speaking in low tones about how strange and wonderful it was to see everyone still alive, still here.

Eventually, only Dougie, June, Karen, Brian, and Maureen remained.

"Come on, love," June said to Karen. "We're heading home. Say goodbye."

Karen hugged everyone, more attached to these "aunties" and "uncles" than she'd admit. "We should do this every year," she declared.

"We'll need bigger chairs," Barry called from the kitchen.

After they left, Maureen turned to Brian.

"I should be going," she said. "Got a room over near the station. Long day tomorrow with solicitors and all that."

"Can I walk you there?" Brian asked.

She hesitated. Then nodded. "Just like old times," she said.

"Not quite," he answered. "But close enough."

They left together through the side gate, footsteps fading into the quiet street.

THE MEDWAY YEARS

Dougie watched them go, June leaning into his side.

"You all right?" she asked.

"I think so," he said. "Feels like a chapter closing. But not in a sad way."

"In what way then?"

"In a... 'to be continued' way," he said.

June smiled. "I can live with that."

CHAPTER FORTY-TWO – "The River Again"

Later that night, after June and Karen had gone to bed, Dougie took a solitary walk down to the river.

Old habit. Old comfort.

The air was cool, the water dark and steady. He leaned on the railing, hands clasped, and let memories roll over him like the tide.

The Riverview dance hall. Laughter on Saturday nights. Tony and Maggie. Kevin and June. Brian and Maureen. Brenda's mischief. Martin's jokes. Barry's steady presence.

The fights. The tears. The heartbreaks.

The jobs gained and lost. The drinks poured and put down. The letters that crossed oceans. The babies born. The loves that fell apart and those that once seemed lost but weren't.

THE MEDWAY YEARS

They were all in there, somewhere, folded into the years.

He wasn't a boy anymore. None of them were.

But he felt an odd peace in that. They had survived. They had grown. They had made mistakes and carried scars and found happiness in places they never expected.

He took a deep breath of the river air.

He knew that Maureen would soon board a plane back to Canada. Back to the life she'd built there, back to her responsibilities. But he also knew she wouldn't be going alone in the way she once had.

She and Brian had exchanged addresses, numbers, promises that were slower and more careful than when they were young—but stronger because of it.

They might write. They might visit. They might find a way to make something new out of something old.

Or they might not. But the possibility was there now. And sometimes that was enough.

CHAPTER FORTY-THREE – "What Remains"

In the months that followed:

Tony and Sarah celebrated a small, happy wedding anniversary with dinner at the same Italian restaurant where he'd once stared trembling at a glass of wine and chosen to stay standing.

THE MEDWAY YEARS

Kevin continued coaching, occasionally bringing Danny to see "Uncle Dougie" and "Auntie June," the boy half-aware that his father's stories of wild youth were more truth than fiction.

Barry and Jackie's home remained the unofficial hub, birthdays and small gatherings held there, always with extra chairs "just in case."

Brenda took a job at the dock office, her sea days fewer now, her stories far more numerous. She visited Martin regularly, dragging him out for walks and making him laugh in a way that reminded everyone of the boy he'd been.

Brian returned to Kuwait for a shorter contract, but not before posting a letter to Canada.

He waited weeks for the reply. When it came, he sat with it on his lap for a long time before opening it.

Dear Brian, it was good to see you. Strange, but good. I don't know where this goes, if anywhere. But I know now that the door isn't closed. That's enough for today. Write again. Love,
Maureen.

And he did.

Again, and again.

The Atlantic no longer felt as wide.

THE MEDWAY YEARS

EPILOGUE – "The Medway Years"

Years later, when Karen was grown and living in London, she came home one weekend and found Dougie sitting at the kitchen table, an old photograph album open in front of him.

"Dad?" she said. "What's that?"

He smiled. "History, love."

She sat beside him. He turned the pages.

Grainy photos at The Riverview dance hall. Lads in suits, girls in dresses. The river. The old football pitch. Laughing faces, some she recognised, some she only knew through stories.

"Who's that?" she asked, pointing to one.

"That's Tony," Dougie said. "Before the years caught up with him. And that's Kevin. And Brian. And there—" he tapped the edge of another photo— "that's Maureen, visiting from Canada."

"You all look so young," Karen said, half-amused, half-awed.

"We were," Dougie replied. "And we thought it would last forever."

"Did it?" she asked.

He considered.

"In a way," he said. "Not the dancing and the late nights and the foolish things we did. Those stopped. But the important

THE MEDWAY YEARS

bits—the friendships, the way we cared about each other, the way those years shaped who we became… that lasted."

She leaned her head on his shoulder. "You miss it?" she asked.

"Sometimes," he said. "But I don't wish to go back. I like knowing how it all turned out."

"How did it?" she asked. "Turn out, I mean."

Dougie closed the album, resting his hand on the cover.

"We made it," he said simply. "Not perfectly. Not without regrets. But we made it. We loved, we broke, we mended. We found our ways."

He looked out of the window where June was hanging washing, sunlight catching in her hair.

"That's all any of us can really ask for," he added. "A life you can look back on and think—*yes. That was mine. And I lived it.*"

Karen smiled.

"You should write it down," she said. "All of it."

Dougie chuckled.

"Maybe one day," he said.

And as the afternoon light poured into the kitchen, full of quiet dust motes and the murmurs of a house that had seen its share of joy and sorrow, he thought— Maybe he would.

After all, some stories deserved to be told properly.

THE MEDWAY YEARS

Especially the ones that began in Medway, in the early 1960s, when the future seemed endless and the river flowed silently past, carrying their youth away but never quite their memories.

And that, he knew, would always be with him.

The years had carried them far, but somehow they had found their way back—like tides returning home to the Medway shore.

Table of Contents

THE MEDWAY YEARS

THE MEDWAY YEARS

BOOK DESCRIPTION

Medway, 1961. A group of working-class teenagers grow up together in the shadow of the River Medway—dancing at Riverview Hall, dreaming beyond the dockyard in Chatham, and believing adulthood will be simple.

THE MEDWAY YEARS

Life proves them wrong.

Dougie and June build a steady life from fragile beginnings.

Kevin's football dreams collapse under jealousy and anger before he fights his way to redemption.

Tony spirals into alcoholism after heartbreak, then slowly rebuilds his life with the help of AA and a gentle new love.

Brenda finds freedom in the Royal Navy.

Martin battles demons he can't laugh away.

Barry and Jackie become the group's quiet anchor.

Brian and Maureen are pulled apart by circumstance—he to Kuwait, she to Canada—never quite extinguishing the love they shared.

By 1980, scattered by decades of choices, the old gang reunites at a summer garden party. Memories rise, wounds reopen and hopes rekindle—especially when Brian and Maureen meet again and discover their feelings never truly faded.

The Medway Years is a moving story of friendship, heartbreak, second chances, and the way our earliest bonds shape us long after youth has gone.

Printed in Great Britain
by Amazon

392155e4-6e23-4fb9-ad75-6bff772ebc8aR01